FREAK!
A Love Story

BY A.L. RUSSELL

Copyright © 2023 A.L. Russell

All rights reserved.

ISBN: 9798393254797

ACKNOWLEDGEMENT

To Nada Bizic-Teague - Only you could have transformed my briar's nest into a rose garden, and for that, I am truly grateful!

To Lexy for taking my vision of my book cover and bringing it to life.

ACKNOWLEDGMENTS

When my novel, *Freak, A Love Story,* was conceived, I grappled with whether I should publish it under a pen name or not. I really wanted to spread my wings and fly, but not get them clipped either, if you know what I mean.

Let me assure you that I was not ashamed or embarrassed about the subject matter I chose to write about, not at all. The relationship between two people in love is a beautiful and natural thing. The main reason I chose this route was to prevent stepping on anyone's toes.

There are all kinds of love, but what love would you describe as the most valued love of all? To me, it's the love of a mother for her child. That I would consider the most treasured of them all. This is the love that shapes us from the moment of conception until that life takes its first breath, and that wet and squirming little being is placed upon the breast.

That moment still takes my breath away even now just thinking about it after all of these years. The pain of childbirth is an inherited debt, but that very debt, through all its misery, still provides so much joy!

But, what if that's not the case at all? *Freak, A Love Story* provides you with a raw and debilitating view of how a genetic defect at birth descends my protagonist down the proverbial "rabbit hole" towards madness.

PROLOUGE

Twenty-year-old Geraldine Peterson had a big problem. No matter how hard she tried to wish it away, it was not happening, and she desperately needed help. She knocked on Ms. Gracie's door, lightly at first, but when that next contraction hit her, she started to bang even harder.

Ms. Gracie was old and tired, but Geraldine's only hope and just about the only person in the tenement housing projects with some kind of transportation.

"Who is it?" she yelled through the door. "It's me, Ms. Gracie, Geraldine Peterson. Please Ms. Gracie, I need your help bad." That's when the door opened - just a crack.

"Ms. Gracie, please, could you take me to the county hospital? If you could just drop me off, I'll be fine. You wouldn't have to wait. I don't think I can make it on foot."

"Damn girl, why you wait 'til this time of the night to have that damn baby? How long you been in pain?"

"All day, Ms. Gracie."

"Then you shoulda got out of here before now. Damn, girl, I'm too old and tired for all this excitement. You got any gas money because neither of us is going to get too far if you don't."

"Yes ma'am." She handed her a twenty Baah had given her the last time she saw him, and she knew not to ask for some of it back. "Damn girl, let's go."

Geraldine crawled into the back seat just as the next contraction ripped through her so hard it felt like someone sucker punched her in the lower part of her belly. It hurt her so much she couldn't even cry.

"Has your water broken yet?" she asked as she made a sharp turn around the corner, almost throwing Geraldine out of the seat. "Ma'am?" Geraldine had no idea what she was talking about. except when she peed on herself this morning and had blood in her panties when she went to the bathroom.

"Did the doctor give you any idea when you were due?"

"No, ma'am. I been intending to go to the doctor, but I just kept putting it off."

"Girl, Lord have mercy! Let me hurry up and get you to this hospital without getting pulled over by the police, heaven forbid."

Geraldine tried to hold back, but all of a sudden, a pain hit her so hard that a horrendous scream tore through her throat, mimicking the pain that tore through her vagina, and that's when she saw the lights of the emergency room entrance to the hospital.

Ms. Gracie got out of the car and came around and opened the door to the back seat. An emergency room attendant came out with a gurney. "Her baby is coming," she heard Ms. Gracie tell him. "Call me girl and let me know how you doin', and I'll come back and pick you up." That's the last thing Geraldine remembered.

The sun sitting high in the sky cast the most

wonderful sense of calm over Geraldine when she opened her eyes. She placed her hand firmly against her belly. "Well, at least that part was over," she said quietly to herself, barely above a whisper. But where was it? This definitely wasn't the maternity ward at Cook County Hospital. Maybe she died and went to a better place. Maybe they both did, and that would be a good thing.

She managed to sit herself up on the side of the bed, but she hurt all over. Well, one thing was for sure, she was still amongst the living because there was no pain and suffering in heaven.

Just as she attempted to try and stand, one of the nurses stuck her head in the door. "Oh, you're finally awake," she said. "Let me get your chart." The nurse returned quickly which was a surprise.

"Geraldine Peterson?"

"Did my baby die?" Geraldine asked.

"No, Ms. Peterson."

"Then where is it?" Geraldine wondered why she was in a private room.

Geraldine's questions seemed to leave the nurse unprepared to answer, and she began to look through Geraldine's chart.

"Well, Dr. Avery was the attending physician during your baby's birth, and he wants to be notified as soon as you're awake."

"Did something go wrong?" Geraldine asked. She had to admit, she didn't remember much.

"Let me page Dr. Avery and let him know you are awake, how's that?"

"That's fine, but what did I have, a boy or a girl?"

"I'm not sure," she said, being noticeably evasive but she wasn't the nurse on duty last night when Geraldine was brought in. "It doesn't say in your chart that there were any complications. Just lay back and relax Ms. Peterson. I will page Dr. Avery right away. He's right here in the hospital. Are you hungry or thirsty?" she asked Geraldine. She was trying hard to avoid any more of Geraldine's questions.

"Just thirsty," Geraldine managed to say, and that was just the opportunity she needed to escape so she didn't have to answer any more questions. When she returned, she had Dr. Avery with her.

"Good evening, Ms. Peterson. I'm Dr. Avery, the attending physician who delivered your baby. "How are you feeling?" he asked.

"I'll feel better when you tell me what's going on. It's obvious that something is, so just say it." He pulled up a chair and sat down. "Yes, Ms. Peterson, there is a problem. The nurse is bringing the baby up from the nursery as we speak." The baby was rolled into the room in one of those small rolling cribs. Dr. Avery stood and lifted the baby out and placed it in Geraldine's arms. It was the most beautiful thing Geraldine had ever seen, with that dark chocolate skin, just like Baah's, her baby's father, and those beautiful bright eyes which held you captive in their embrace.

"Ms. Peterson, your baby was born with a very rare birth defect called Hermaphroditism."

"Her what?" Geraldine was completely unfamiliar with the term. "What is that?"

Dr. Avery unwrapped the baby from its blanket and removed its diaper. "Your baby's condition is called True Hermaphroditism. These babies are born with both fully functioning sex organs." When Geraldine's eyes focused on the horror of what she was seeing, she screamed so loudly, you could hear her all over the entire ward.

"Get it away from me." she screamed. "That's disgusting, an abomination," almost shoving the baby off onto the floor and Dr. Avery catching it just in time.

The nurse immediately carried the baby from the room screaming just as loudly as Geraldine was from the shock of what she had just learned.

"So, what you're trying to tell me is that thing is a boy *and* a girl?" as she was still shrieking.

When the nurse came back into the room without the baby, Dr. Avery asked her to give Ms. Peterson something to calm her down while he desperately tried to explain this very complicated act of nature, which was no one's fault, not hers, not the father's, and definitely not the infant's.

The nurse returned soon after and gave Geraldine an injection, and whatever it was, Geraldine welcomed it. Maybe if she went to sleep when she woke up, all of this would be just a bad dream.

Geraldine turned over on her side and faced the wall, but Dr. Avery did not go away. "Ms. Peterson, please try to listen," he said calmly. He knew this was almost impossible for her to wrap her brain around because True Hermaphroditism was very rare. "There are only six to seven hundred cases worldwide, and most of them are in South Africa. Just rest, Ms. Peterson. I intend to make sure that you and your newborn receive the very best physical and psychological support needed to see you through this difficult time, and I will be with you every step of the way. You are not alone, Ms. Peterson."

Geraldine lay there with her back turned, but her eyes were wide open, and she finally spoke. "So, it is a boy and a girl?"

"Yes, Ms. Peterson, for now, it is."

"Then she will be a girl, and her name will be Anne, Anne Marie Peterson. Before she let the medication take her away, the last thing she chose to remember was South Africa where Baah, her baby's father, was born. That's when all the hate and bitterness began to fester inside Geraldine Peterson like a boil releasing all its poison.

FORTY-FIVE YEARS LATER, ST. LOUIS, MISSOURI

Anne Marie Peterson has a secret. A secret she has lived with since the day she was born, and she would take to her grave if she had any choice in the matter, but there is just one problem. It only takes one other person to know the secret, and then it's no longer a secret anymore. The one person you would think you could trust with a secret so personal, so life-changing, would be your own mother, but sometimes that's not always the case.

1

Anne was slowly losing her grip on reality. She could feel it, and the sad part of it all was that she didn't know how to stop it. After she arrived at work and parked, she felt such comfort just sitting in her car. Lately, the smaller her surroundings, the safer she felt, like being wrapped in a cocoon. Lord have mercy. What was happening to her?

Anne sat in her car for the longest time, and finally, she had to force herself to turn the motor off and open the door. There was a briskness in the air that gave her some connection with normalcy, and she held onto it for dear life.

The season was starting to change, and like the changing season, the day would get better as the day moved forward, but right now, she felt so vulnerable and so exposed. Sometimes, secrets can make you feel like the whole world knows what you're hiding. Recently, she had started getting to work earlier. Idle chatter first thing after arriving at work made it difficult for her to act normally, but by the time everyone else got there, she would be settled in and better able to function.

She could hear Sharon talking and laughing with Chrystal down the hall. Anne liked Sharon a lot and She didn't want to do anything to disappoint her or give her any reason to question her work performance. Anne had never felt confident about herself, but lately, she felt even more inadequate. With all the other crazy stuff going on with her, she desperately wanted it all to just go away.

Finally, Sharon made her way to Anne's office. "Good morning, Ms. Anne," she said with her beautiful smile. "And good morning to you, too," Anne said, returning the smile.

Anne felt like she was functioning on a very short fuse, and she hated it.

Sharon was so funny and sure of herself, but she was also very sensitive to others as well. She had a way about her that made a person feel important.

"Anne, is everything okay with you?" she asked while closing the door behind her sensing the unexpected.

"I'm okay," Anne said, trying to keep things cool. "Just trying to work through some things, but other than that, I'm fine."

"Anne, you know what you should do today? Why don't you get out of the office and do something different for a change of pace?"

Anne could feel Sharon's excitement building, especially when she came up with what she thought was a great idea. "Or, I have another idea. I know you like Louise, and I know Louise likes working with you as well. I'm thinking it would be a great idea if you were to go down and work with Louise today. They have been so short-staffed down there in some of the other departments, and she asked for you specifically, that is, if we could spare you."

Anne tried her best to focus on what Sharon was saying, but her voice seemed to be getting further and further away. She felt like someone had put a plastic bag over her head, and every time she tried to take a breath, she was suffocating.

Thank goodness Anne's office chair was directly behind her because without any warning, she lost consciousness and Sharon had to gently assist her into the chair as she went limp.

Anne felt like she was in a completely dark place. She could feel Sharon beside her, but she could not see her face.

"Sharon, please don't make me go down there. I'll do anything if you just let me stay right here."

Anne was holding onto Sharon so tightly; she could feel her heartbeat. She tried hard to free herself from this nightmare and whatever was happening to her, but she could no longer hide it.

Fear, shame, and desperation were overtaking Anne, and she sobbed uncontrollably.

For some unknown reason, Anne had this overwhelming fear that if Sharon sent her to work with Louise, and away from her safety net she would be lost and just the thought terrified her. "Sharon, I can't go down there. If you send me down there, I will be lost." Sharon didn't know what to do or say.

"Lost how, Anne?"

Anne tried desperately to make sense of what was happening to her but she couldn't and now what was reality and what was a nightmare was exposing her as the "Freak she was. Anne's whole body seemed to convulse.

Sharon wanted desperately to make whatever was happening to Anne go away, and as tightly as Anne was holding on to her, Sharon was tightly holding on to Anne.

It was as if their very lives depended on not letting go. Sharon whispered ever so softly into Anne's ear like a mother comforting her child. She reassured Anne that she didn't have to go anywhere she did not want to go, anywhere at all. "Anne, don't you know that?" she said with such conviction.

Sharon's breath caressed the side of Anne's face like a warm summer's breeze, and the sound of her voice took Anne to a place she had never been before, and that was a place of peace.

Sharon knew she had to get Anne away from the workplace. It was imperative that she did. She picked up the phone and called Chrystal's desk. Chrystal was the department's receptionist.

"Chrystal, Anne is going to be out of the building for part of the day. Do you think you could monitor her calls until she gets back?"

"Sure, Sharon. Just let me know when she gets back, okay?"

"Chrystal, that would be great, and thank you so much."

Sharon went over to Anne and took her by the hand. "Anne, let's get away from here for a while. Would you like that?"

Anne tried to speak, but she couldn't. It was like she had lost her voice as well as her sanity.

All she could do was nod her head in agreement. When they got to Sharon's car, Anne curled up into a tight ball, and Sharon helped secure her seat belt. They drove around for a while not going anywhere in particular, and neither spoke.

Finally, Sharon asked Anne if she was hungry, and she said that she wasn't. "But aren't you Sharon?" she asked with such concern. Sharon assured her that she wasn't hungry either, and she headed out to the lake.

Anne loved it out there, but of course, Sharon knew that because that's the location Anne would always pick for their company's picnic every year.

It was so beautiful. Sharon parked and said nothing about what happened earlier. She got out and came around to

Anne's side of the car and opened the door. "Please come with me, Anne," she requested, holding out her hand.

They walked down to the water's edge and sat in the freshly cut grass. The soft breeze pushed the sun's rays back and forth through the trees and carried the ever-so-soft whisper of Sharon's voice against Anne's skin. Anne had never experienced such tenderness from another person, ever, and she never wanted it to end. A calmness seemed to come over Anne giving her a welcomed sense of relief and peace, even if only for just this little while.

Finally, Sharon suggested that they should head back to work, and Anne agreed but in her heart, Anne wished that they could have stayed that way forever.

Before Sharon went back to her office, she got so close to Anne, looking deep into Anne's eyes searching for answers. The pain and the sadness were so apparent, and it broke Sharon's heart.

"Please don't shut me out, Anne. I will always be here for you, just talk to me." The close proximity of Sharon made Anne gasp for breath, and she backed away.

When Sharon got back to her office, she closed her door and cried. She had never felt so deeply connected to any other person as she did Anne, and it left her feeling bewildered. She had no idea what was happening to Anne, but whatever it was, it was not good, not good at all and it scared her to death that Anne might be having some kind of mental breakdown.

Anne was an excellent employee and a wonderful

person, and Sharon would do whatever it took to protect her, but first she had to get to the core of what was happening to her. But how without causing another incident?

Sharon heard a gentle knock on her door, and she quickly grabbed a tissue and wiped her eyes. When she saw Anne standing there, a wave of relief came over her.

"Come, sit down, Anne." Anne's voice was still weak, but she felt strongly that she needed to tell Sharon how sorry she was about the day. She could not leave without saying something.

She acknowledged that she had not been herself lately and admitted that she had not slept for several days. Anne wanted Sharon to know that she didn't ever have to worry about her work performance, and that she could never disappoint her.

"Please Sharon, don't tell anyone about what happened today." It devastated Sharon to see Anne this way, and she had to calm her fears.

"Anne, whatever is happening to you is between just the two of us and no one else. I would never do anything like that Anne, and by the way, you never have to worry about your position here at The Company either." She begged Anne, "Please Anne, whatever it is, let me help you. We can fix it together."

Anne didn't know what had been happening to her these last few weeks, but one thing she did know was that no one could fix what was wrong with her, no one. Over the years, she learned to accept the things she could not change because she was beyond repair.

Sharon could hear the defeat in Anne's words, and she could see it in her eyes but Most of all, she could feel Anne's pain in her own heart because it was breaking for Anne.

Before Anne left for the day, she knew what she had to do. It was time for her to take a break and until she got her emotions under control, she would never let anything like this happen to her again. She waited for Sharon to leave for the day, and then she placed a leave of absence slip and a note on Sharon's desk.

She knew Sharon didn't understand what was happening to her, but neither did she. And that's why she had to have this time away. The only thing Anne knew for sure was that until she faced the demons that haunted her, she would not survive, and she'd come too far to turn back now.

In her note, she thanked Sharon for being there for her. No one had ever been there for her in her entire life. She was only taking two weeks, and she asked Sharon to please forgive her for doing this on such short notice, but what was she to do?

Life had come to a crossroads for Anne, but where was she to go from here?

The next morning, Sharon awoke anxiously. If only she could get Anne to trust her enough to let her help. She had to do something to get Anne to open up to her.

When she got to her office and sat down at her desk, she immediately saw the leave of absence form and the note from Anne on her desk. Sharon's emotions flooded her from all directions. This was the last thing she expected Anne to do.

She read and reread Anne's note trying to make some sense of the sudden change in their lives. She had nothing left to do but approve Anne's time off and count her blessings that she had only asked for two weeks.

Anne was one of those employees that never took time off, so she could have easily taken over three months if she had wanted to and still had time to spare.

Anne's absence for the next two weeks would put Sharon in an awkward position with her other staff wanting to know what was wrong with her. Was she sick, but most of all, when would she be coming back? There were a lot of questions Sharon didn't have the answers to.

By the end of the day, Sharon decided she had to try to reach out to Anne. Even if she didn't get an answer, she could still leave her a voice message. Sharon was so anxious.

"Hi Anne, she just wanted to let you know that she had approved her time off. Take as much time as you need, but I miss you so much already. Please come back soon."

Sharon sat for the longest time, hoping Anne would pick up the phone, but finally, she hung up. She could not imagine what Anne was going through by trying to keep up the farce that everything was fine when clearly things were not fine at all.

Anne hung on to Sharon's every word, and she wondered if she had made a mistake leaving Sharon to cover for her with her other staff. She knew Sharon was worried about her, and it hurt her that she didn't have the courage to talk to her. Having someone like Sharon care about whether she lived or died was scary for Anne, but if she ever knew the truth about her, she would be disgusted. She could not bear that kind of rejection from her.

Anne listened to Sharon's message again. Hearing her voice gave Anne much comfort, and she needed her so badly.

SHARON

It had been only a week since Sharon last talked to Anne, but it felt like forever. She didn't know how she would get through another week. She missed Anne so much.

Sharon couldn't understand what could be so bad that Anne couldn't share it with her. Maybe she just needed to get a life, she scolded herself, then she wouldn't be so wrapped up in someone else's business.

Everyone thought Sharon had so much going for her, and that she could have the pick of any man she wanted, but that's what her problem was. She had never found that special someone who rocked her boat, so she feared that at thirty years old, she probably had her expectations set way too high.

Sharon never came close to marriage and having children. This was never a priority for her either. She had never had sex, and she always kept men at arm's length.

Giving up her virginity to just anyone was out of the question. She would know when the time was right.

Without giving it a second thought, she picked up the phone and dialed Anne's number. "How dare you, Anne?" she said practically yelling into the phone. She presumed she wouldn't get an answer, but she sure could give her a piece of her mind.

"CHICKEN!!!!! How dare you ignore me this way Anne when you know how worried I am about you? You have twenty-four hours to get your ass back to work or let me help you. Anne, please." Then this long silence. It was like Sharon was waiting for Anne to pick up, and Anne waiting for Sharon to hang up. Sharon cried. She hurt so badly.

The next morning Sharon was not herself. She called into work and told a lie about why she was going to be late. "Chrystal, good morning."

"Good morning, Sharon."

She told Chrystal she had to take her car to the shop, and she would be there as soon as she was done. Chrystal assured her there was no problem, and that she would hold down the fort until she was able to get there.

"Thanks, Chrystal."

It was getting harder every day since Anne had been gone for Sharon to be her typical easy-going self, and she felt she had pretty much blown things with Anne. Getting her head together was the hardest thing she ever had to do.

Anne and Sharon seemed to be sharing the same boat lately, and Sharen didn't know what was happening with her own emotional state either. All she knew was that she was miserable, and by the time she got to work, it was 1:00 p.m. She was one haggard mess. Now, if she could just manage not to show it was the problem.

She stopped and chatted with Chrystal like she usually did. "Girl, this car of mine is beginning to turn into a piece of junk." Chrystal laughed. "I know that's the truth," she said. "Yours and mine."

"Yeah well, it might as well get it together because there will be no replacing it anytime soon," and they both laughed. "Later girl," and Sharon headed down the hall to her office.

When Sharon opened the door to her office and saw Anne standing there, her legs felt weak. "I got your message, so here I am." Anne said. Sharon closed the door behind her, and their eyes stayed locked on to the another's. Sharon came so close to Anne when she embraced her that her lips brushed ever so lightly against hers, and it was like a revelation.

No longer was there any doubt about what was happening between them, and Anne knew she had no other choice but to tell Sharon the truth about herself.

"Please don't let me lose you when I do, "was the silent echo in Anne's head. Sharon asked Anne if she could come by her place after work.

"I will be waiting," she said, and they parted without

another word. Anne managed to come and go without being seen by anyone, and that was a good thing. Until they could put their heads together and figure out what was happening between them, they both knew that Anne needed to be gone one more.

2

When Anne left Sharon's office, they both knew the challenges they would be facing, but none of that mattered as long as they would be together.

The rest of the day was like a dream they both were participating in at the same time, and their imaginations consumed them in anticipation, but also in fear of the unknown. When Sharon left work that evening, she went to Anne's, not looking to be perfectly put together or any of the things that used to mean so much to her, but just as she was, pure and unspoiled by anyone else.

When Anne opened the door, the sight of Sharon made her breath catch in her throat. Neither of them spoke. Sometimes, words are the last thing two people need between each other.

Anne had always thought Sharon was attractive, but her beauty was intoxicating. She truly was beautiful on the inside and out.

Neither of them had ever felt like this about anyone

before, and they wanted the feeling to last forever. The soft smooth melody of the music playing in the background seemed to drift in and out like the ocean tides taking all their worries out to sea with them.

The next morning when Sharon opened her eyes, she was curled up on one end of the sofa and Anne was sitting on the other watching her sleep. She had retrieved a pillow from her bed and covered Sharon with a light cover.

"Anne, did you get any rest at all?" Sharon asked. "Yes, some, but I'm not tired at all, Sharon. If truth be told, I was afraid if I slept, I would wake up and all of this would have been a dream."

"Well, it is not a dream Anne, Sharon assured her and she wasn't going anywhere."

They stood there, neither of them wanting to let go of that most wonderful feeling of belonging. But as much as Sharon hated to, she would have to leave so she would have enough time to stop at her place and change clothes for work. Without saying anything, Anne placed a folded piece of paper in Sharon's hand with the word Hermaphrodite. "This is what I am, Sharon, and if I don't hear from you again, I will understand." They parted without another word.

When Sharon got to work, she sat at her desk holding the folded piece of paper Anne had given her but had never opened. Whatever was written on the paper would never change how she felt about Anne, so she destroyed it without ever reading it.

'THANK GOD IT'S FRIDAY! Today, Sharon did the

unusual. She worked through her lunch break and left early. She had plans. She stopped at her place, grabbed a couple of steaks, a bottle of wine, salad fixings, and was standing on Anne's doorstep in less than an hour. No call ahead, no worries, or any of that. This weekend belonged to them.

It was only when she rang the doorbell that she briefly thought, "What if Anne wasn't home?" That thought went right out with the breeze when Anne opened the door.

"Can I come in, Anne?" she asked. If this is love, she thought to herself, please don't ever let it go away. Anne quickly closed the door behind her. "Let the rest of the world go away," Anne thought to herself, and she followed Sharon's lead.

They headed to the kitchen, and when Sharon came close to Anne, she could hardly bear it. She let the music work its magic while her body moved with a rhythm all its own.

"Do you like to dance, Anne?" she asked. When Anne took her in her arms, her whole body trembled as they swayed to the music. Sharon's skin was the color of raw honey, pure and untampered with just like she was.

Anne knew that no one else but her had ever seen this side of Sharon before, and that's why she would never do anything to hurt her.

They spent the most wonderful evening together, laughing and rough housing and sipping on wine. Reluctantly, Sharon knew she should give Anne some space. She didn't want to impose on her any more than she had already, and she told Anne that, but Anne didn't want Sharon to leave. All her life she had been so alone, and just the thought of losing Sharon now would destroy her.

Anne was so confused by what was happening to her. She knew nothing about her own body except it was not normal, and she was not normal, but the way Sharon made her feel felt so normal. It was like nothing she had ever experienced, and the thought of losing that feeling scared Anne beyond measure.

She didn't want to do anything to scare Sharon away, but she said, "Sharon, please don't leave." She could not go another day without telling her the truth about what she really was, even if that truth could destroy her. She was so scared.

"Sharon, did you read the note I gave you this morning when you were here?" There was a long silence between them that made Anne's heart hurt. Sharon moved so close to Anne that she felt like she was losing her mind. She snuggled her soft skin against Anne's face and whispered ever so softly in her ear.

"I've never been with anyone before, Anne. Have you? I'm a virgin. "Are you Anne? When the time comes, please be gentle." Anne didn't know what to do or say, but there was only one thing that mattered more than anything else and that was the two of them would be doing it together.

Sharon stood on her tippy toes and kissed Anne softly on the lips. "Would it be okay if I come back tomorrow?" she asked, even though she already knew the answer. Anne barely moved her mouth away from Sharon's, savoring the sweet warm caress of her breath against hers. Is this what he had been starving for since the day he was born?

The next morning, Anne woke up to a ringing phone, and for a moment, it brought back terrifying memories that chilled him to the core. "Good morning, Anne. I'm on my way if that's okay."

"Yes." He would be ready when she got here, he said to himself, almost breathless. He was up and out of the bed so fast you would have thought he had just received a shot of adrenaline. He didn't know what Sharon had planned, and it really didn't matter as long as they were together.

The only way Anne could describe how Sharon had affected him was to compare it to a dead person who had been raised back to life. It may sound strange, but all of Anne's life he felt as if he had never existed at all, and feelings like this were all a part of his paranoia. He would always wake up to the reality that it was just a cruel joke, and the joke was always on him. How sad. No one should ever be made to feel so unnecessary.

When the doorbell rang and Anne opened the door, reality stepped up and slapped him right in the face. "Going somewhere?" came the voice standing behind Sharon. This startled Sharon because she was unaware that someone had walked up behind her without acknowledging their presence.

Oh my God, it was Anne's mother! "What are you

doing here, mom, and how did you find me?"

"Find you… have you been hiding?" she said in a cowardly way. Sharon finally found her voice. "Oh, my goodness," Sharon said. "You startled me. Good morning, Ms. Peterson," she said politely.

"Good morning, Ms. Pretty. Anne, who is your friend?"

Anne's terrifying memories had just become a reality. "Mom, we were just on our way out," she said, trying to escape this nightmare. Anne hadn't seen her mother since she was eighteen years old, and for her to just appear without any warning left Anne feeling weak and frail.

She introduced Sharon. "Mom, this is my supervisor, Sharon, and we were just on our way out. Can we talk later?" she managed to say.

"Wow, Anne. Your supervisor is hot. You could sure take a few pointers from her," she said in a belittling tone.

Anne's mom backed them inside and made herself comfortable.

Anne tried to not let her being there intimidate her, but it still did after all these years. "We only have a minute, mom."

"So, the two of you work together," she continued, ignoring Anne's plea of time. "That's great. Have the two of you been on your job a long time?" she asked. "Sharon, you look awfully young to be a supervisor," completely dismissing Anne. "How long have you known each other?"

Sharon told her that she has known her daughter for a very long time, that Anne is a very good friend, that Anne is a good person, and that she likes her very much.

Out of nowhere, she said. "Anne, have you told your good friend Sharon about yourself yet?"

"Told me what exactly, Ms. Peterson?" Sharon shot back.

"Anne, you've been holding out on your good friend, Sharon," as Ms. Peterson was really enjoying watching Anne squirm. Sharon could see what this was doing to Anne, and she did not like it one bit. Anne tried to find her voice, but her mother was having too much fun at the expense of her own child.

"Well Anne, it's obvious you still need your old momma's help. Anne has never been able to come clean about what she really is, Ms. Sharon," as she snickered delightfully as she quipped.

Suddenly, Sharon was like a momma bear protecting her cub. "Look, Mom." Sharon sounded like a completely different person, and now it was Anne's mother who was caught completely off guard.

"Ms. Peterson, whatever you're trying to insinuate about Anne…. Sorry, you'll have to forgive us. I would have hoped to meet you under better circumstances, but like Anne said before, we are on our way out, and so are you." all the while escorting her out and locking the door behind them. Sharon had Anne by the hand, and left Anne's mother standing there with her mouth open.

After they had driven a short distance, Sharon pulled over and parked.

An invisible dark cloud completely consumed Anne, and the look in his eyes was the look of a completely broken and down-trodden spirit. Sharon's heart felt so heavy in her chest, she could hardly speak. "How dare she continue to hurt you anymore than she already has, Anne "but " Not on my watch," she said in no uncertain terms.

Anne could hear the anger in Sharon's words, and she couldn't help but smile. She had just witnessed one of the many sides of Sharon Grayson today that she didn't know existed. They sat there, so quietly and Sharon could tell that Anne was no longer present. The thought of his mother being here after all these years was like being transported back to another place in time where his nightmares began and still existed, and as long as Geraldine Peterson was around, it would not end well.

Anne could hear Sharon's voice off in the distance calling his name like the day this nightmare began. "Anne, are you okay?" Sharon turned in her seat and faced Anne, and when she gently caressed the back of Anne's neck, she flinched. "My dear, sweet Anne, life has not been kind, has it?"

The touch of Sharon's hand against Anne's skin and the comforting sound of her voice brought Anne back to reality. "Yes, I'm okay, Sharon," but she could see the fear and hopelessness in Anne's eyes that she so desperately wanted to hide.

      Sharon started the car and drove around for a while, and then headed back to Anne's place. It was time for them to talk.

3

Anne could tell Sharon was restless, and she wanted to touch her so bad, but she dared not. "Sharon, please come and sit down, "Anne said softly, but Sharon's emotions were all over the place but So were Anne's.

Sharon said, "Anne, how do I make you feel when we're together?" Anne wasn't sure what she meant when she asked him how she made him feel, because his own body felt like it had taken on a mind of its own that he no longer had any control of. Sharon was a woman in every way, but she sensed something was going on with Anne, and she wanted him to admit it. "Say what you're feeling, Anne."

Anne tried to change the direction the conversation was going, but when Sharon stood in the middle of the living room floor and let her dress drop to the floor, she was daring Anne to keep his hands to himself. Anne had never seen something so beautiful in his life.

Her breasts were like fruit ripened by the sun, the

color of raw honey. And her pubic hair was just a faint growth of the most beautiful deep brown that matched the color of the hair on her head perfectly. Her belly tapered down and merged into her faint fuzz that made you want to bury your face in it. This woman was perfect. Anne's body reacted in a way that made him gasp for breath.

"Now, Anne, how does it make you feel when you look at me?" She walked over to Anne and pressed her naked body against him and kissed him with a passion that demanded his manhood to respond.

What Anne was feeling was not what another woman would feel, but rather, what a man would feel when he wanted to please his woman in every way. Anne picked Sharon up in his arms and carried her to his bed, and when she trembled in his embrace, he knew.

Sharon wrapped her arms around him, buried her face in his neck, and whispered in his ear. "Make love to me, Anne, but please don't hurt me." This woman was driving him crazy. "Sharon." The sound of her name escaped from him like a moan. He had to stop this, his voice, low and deep.

"You make me feel like a man, Sharon. A man who wants to own your beautiful, sweet body, but you already know what you do to me, don't you, Sharon?" She was like an illegal drug pulsing through Anne's body.

Anne knew this was not the time to lose control of the situation, but he knew exactly what to do to please Sharon. He caressed her gently between her legs, never inserting a finger, keeping them flat. She arched her back in pleasure. Sharon was so wet and hot, and just touching her filled Anne with hidden pleasures between a man and a woman he could never have imagined.

When he felt her orgasm pulse beneath his hand, it was like an emotional healing to Anne's soul, and he held it there until it was spent. Anne cradled Sharon in his arms and covered her with the bedding from his bed, neither of them wanting to move.

Finally, Anne spoke. It was time for him to tell Sharon the secret he had lived with all of his life. "I am one of nature's biggest mistakes. I was born with both male and female sex organs, and what the medical professionals call "True Hermaphroditism. Because of this mistake of nature, my mother raised me as a female, a life I was cursed to live out for the rest of my days. A "Freak of nature is what my mother called him frequently, so that's how he viewed himself as well."

When Sharon touched him, she could feel his manhood through his clothing, and Anne gently gripped Sharon's hand. Until he saw a doctor, he would never take her virginity from her, never would he do that.

"I'm in love with you, Anne, and nothing will ever change that," she said softly. Sharon was so overcome with emotion, tears blinded her, but when she fully realized the nightmare Anne had been living all of these years, it broke her heart. How could his own mother hate him so much as to punish him this way?

They fell asleep completely exhausted from the events of the day, and when Anne opened his eyes the next morning and saw Sharon sleeping peacefully beside him, she looked so beautiful, so pure. He vowed he would never take that away from her.

While Sharon was sleeping, Anne went into the bathroom and locked the door. For so long, Anne had never looked at his own body, and he even showered in the dark.

He was well aware that it was there because since the two of them had become so intimate with each other, it had made its presence known. It was past time for him to face what he really was, no matter how shocking it might be.

He removed all of his clothing and stood exposed in front of a full-length mirror. At first, he kept his eyes turned away, but then he forced himself to take a long hard look. He couldn't believe what he was seeing.

Anne stood somewhere between 5'11" and 6' and weighed 180 lbs. which he carried very well. His hair was cut short, which gave it a slightly curly texture. There were no signs of breasts, but even without his penis being erect, it still seemed larger than normal. He knew he would have to be extra careful with Sharon, especially when he became excited.

He closed his eyes and turned away from the mirror not wanting to continue, but knowing he had to. Without looking directly at himself again, he retrieved a hand-held mirror from beneath the sink. He had come too far to turn back now.

He sat down on the toilet and positioned the mirror to expose the part he could not see. Under the base of his penis towards the rear was a perfectly normal vagina. When he inserted a finger, it was tight and restricted, but it was definitely there. Anne felt like a freak and just the thought made him sick.

"What am I?" he whispered to himself. He had become completely overwhelmed by this new person he had suddenly become so familiar with. Looking at himself was like invading someone else's private space. He closed his eyes and turned the hand mirror upside down on the floor.

Anne was not feminine to look at and had a strong masculine body. He had everything he needed to be the kind of man he so desperately wanted to be for Sharon. All of his life, he had viewed himself as unworthy, but now, if it was the last thing he ever did, he was determined to be everything Sharon could ever want in a husband. Until he could do that, he would not rest.

Anne had become so engrossed with trying to salvage some parts of his identity, he had lost all connection with time. He had no idea how long he had been locked away in the bathroom, almost an hour at least, but he still was not done.

He flipped the mirror to the other side that magnified. He had always had trouble with facial hair, and he hated it. Being something he wasn't had taken its toll on Anne, and she, or whatever he was, desperately wanted to find the answers.

The only thing now that gave him any consolation was knowing that the things he was feeling whenever Sharon came close to him were not wrong at all, and last night, he was just responding the way a normal man would have and that was desire.

When Anne finally came out of the bathroom, Sharon was in the kitchen making coffee. "Hi Anne," she said softly. Anne could tell Sharon was anxious about everything by the way she busied herself so it wouldn't be so noticeable, but so was Anne.

"I hope you don't mind me hanging around this morning," Anne said in that sleepy morning voice that he could never get used to hearing, "Plus, I overslept, " she admitted with a smile.

Anne went over to Sharon and lifted her up and sat her on the counter in front of him. She felt weightless. He kissed her slowly letting his tongue explore the inside of her mouth, and she wrapped her arms and legs around him and held on tightly. I love you so much, Anne," she whispered.

"I love you too, Sharon. If only you knew how much." Anne carried Sharon into the living room and sat her down on the sofa. "I'll get the coffee, and then we need to talk." Anne came back with the coffee and for the first time in his life, he felt wanted, but more than anything else, he felt needed.

Now it was time for him to do the asking. "Sharon, I want to know how I make you feel, and how you felt about last night." Anne was anxious to know how Sharon viewed him, and Sharon didn't hesitate. "Strong and powerful, Anne, and yet so gentle - vulnerable. You are someone I could never get enough of Anne. I don't want to overwhelm you, but I feel safe with you, Anne, safe enough to let myself go and be the woman I've longed to be and with the man I want to be with."

When Sharon expressed her feelings to Anne and said she saw him as the man he truly was, it was akin to an emotional healing to Anne's soul.

Sharon continued, "It's not all about sex, either," she said.

Right now, Sharon's body felt like it was in bloom, but until it was time, she would be saving all of her flowers for him. She knew Anne would never let that happen until he had full control of what was happening to both of them because right now, she knew she couldn't.

Sharon snuggled herself on the end of the sofa, and Anne cradled her legs in his lap and massaged them gently. "I used to dream about you touching me and lifting me off my feet like you did earlier, "continuing with her thoughts. Her dreams of Anne were so real, even though during those times, she thought he was a woman. She never thought of him that way.

She asked, "Anne, do you remember the day you saved my life?" Anne told her she would never forget. Sharon repositioned herself on the sofa and remembered it like it was yesterday.

There was a history between the two of them that

joined them years before. A secret not shared. Not even with the other. They both participated in their annual company hiking and fishing trip that everyone looked forward to with so much excitement. To this day, Sharon couldn't remember how it happened. Herself, Louise Russell, and a couple of other women were laughing and joking around when all of a sudden, a huge deer appeared out of nowhere. The deer was so close she could have reached out and touched it. Thinking back now, that's probably how it happened. She remembered screaming when she felt herself falling backwards, but that's the last thing she remembered.

"When I opened my eyes, you were there, Anne, holding me in your arms and brushing my hair back away from my face. All I could do was look deeply into your comforting eyes. There was so much sadness, but also a longing and desire. It was so apparent, Anne. Now I know it was not my imagination," Sharon said softly.

She never thought she could ever feel that way about another woman, but somehow it was different with Anne. The way he touched her awakened something inside of her that she did not know how to deal with. "I think I have always loved you, Anne," finally acknowledging it to herself. That's why she saved herself, never wanting anyone else to touch her.

Listening to the way Sharon expressed herself about the way she felt about him affected Anne profoundly. Anne brushed Sharon's hair back away from her face and ran his finger along the still visible scar along her hairline. The fear of losing her that day, still haunts Anne.

The few times she did date, she had guys say she was frigid, and maybe she was. She actually imagined Anne as her lover, she confessed.

"The way you touched me that day Anne, I knew you would never let anything happen to me. I must have lost consciousness again after that because the next time I opened my eyes, I was in the hospital, and you were still there. I remember seeing the relief in your eyes, but also the love. The nurse said you had been there for two days."

Sharon continued, "A lot of the staff talked about it for a long time, and about how you risked your own life to save mine. They said you carried me up a steep embankment in your arms to a safe place until help arrived. Do you remember that Anne?"

"Yes, Sharon," he remembered.

How can two people be so connected to the other for all this time, and yet, keep it secret – even from the other?

Tomorrow was Monday and a new beginning for both. So much had changed, and Anne couldn't help but worry if he should come back to work early or stay off for the rest of his time. He missed Sharon so much when she was gone, but they both agreed that it was imperative that Anne seek medical attention as soon as possible.

Anne opened a book that was laying on the coffee table and handed Sharon an envelope containing his birth certificate and the attending physician's name who delivered him. This would be as good a place to start as any, and that's even if he was still in practice or even alive after all these years.

    Sharon could see how worried Anne was about everything, and she didn't want him dwelling on the what ifs, so she assured Anne that tomorrow morning when she got to work, she would get on the computer and see if Dr. Avery's medical practice or office was still listed. And if they were lucky enough, maybe she could help him by making him an appointment.

    Sharon leaned back and rested her back against Anne's chest, and Anne's arms immediately encircled her giving them a tender and much-deserved feeling of finally belonging.

    Anne hadn't been to Chicago since he was eighteen years old, and that's when he was accepted into Dr. Robinson's program and was eventually able to escape from the years of emotional abuse inflicted by his mother, as well as his own mind. But had he really?

    Seeing his mother standing there yesterday was like ice water running through his veins, and just thinking about it made Anne want to get as far away from her as possible. Now that Sharon was in the picture, running away was no longer an option for Anne anymore.

    They both knew that their relationship would not be easy, but anything worth having is worth suffering for, and the first step was Dr. Avery. Only he could tell them if Anne had any chance of living a normal life.

    The next morning when Anne woke up, Sharon was already gone, and he felt so lost. They both knew they would have to be extra careful when he did come back to work, but at least being there would fill the void.

When Anne showed up on her lunch break, Anne knew she had found out something she was not comfortable with talking about at work. Anne sat down on the sofa, and Sharon curled up in his lap and laid her head against Anne's chest. "Friday, August 25th at 1:00 p.m. is your appointment with Dr. Avery."

"This Friday, Sharon?"

That was an unexpected surprise Anne had not prepared for. "Honey, if she hadn't secured that appointment, it would have been over a month before you could see him, and that was not an option," Sharon insisted.

Sharon told Dr. Avery that her partner was having some physical as well as psychological problems. Dr. Avery asked Sharon if he had seen the patient before, and she told him yes, because his receptionist had already said he was not taking any new patients. Sharon advised him that the last time he saw him was when he was only two weeks old, and he was the attending physician when he was born. Sharon went on, "Anne, when he asked what the patient's name was and I told him Anne Marie Peterson, honey, the response was, 'Oh my God'."

"Anne, we cannot miss this appointment," Sharon asserted. Anne hated how all of this was disrupting Sharon's life and her position at The Company in her efforts to be morally supportive. She had already given Anne more than he could ever have wished for, and that was her love.

"Please, Sharon, I'm going to be okay," Anne insisted, but of course, Sharon was not listening. "Anne, please don't worry. Just know I have everything under control."

Sharon had given the rest of her staff the okay to leave at noon on Friday. "Everyone has been working so hard while you've been gone, and they deserve this. They are really excited about getting to leave early, especially on Friday."

Sharon went on, "They miss you, Anne, and wanted me to tell you to take as much time as you need, and your position would always be here when you return. Besides, no one wanted it but you anyway, Anne." They both laughed at that one.

None of the staff liked Anne's job because she had to deal a lot with the public, but she had a real rapport with them and the staff hated it when Anne was not available. No matter how challenging the situation could be, Anne would always manage to leave people satisfied, and they would constantly tell Dr. Robinson, the owner, how valuable Anne was to The Company. Anne has been with the company for over twenty-seven years, which was a true testament to her worth as a Company employee.

Sharon snuggled deeper into Anne's arms and seemed to drift off for a moment. "Damn, Anne thought to himself," and wished she could have stayed right where she was. Sharon seemed so much at peace.

The rest of the week seemed to drag. Sharon stayed

at work on her lunch break, and even stayed over a couple of days just to make sure she stayed on top of things, but Anne was miserable. Just lying beside Sharon at night was hard on the both of them.

One night, Sharon forced herself to spend the night back at her own place because Anne's next-door neighbor started becoming nosey, or should it be said, nosier. Both could tell she was wondering why Sharon had started spending so much time at Anne's place, not that it was any of her business.

Sharon was miserable, and she cried most of the night. She didn't sleep, and neither did Anne. They couldn't wait for Friday to come.

4

They arrived in Chicago and had plenty of time to get to Dr. Avery's office. He came out, greeted them, and escorted them back to his office. Dr. Avery never thought in a million years he would ever lay eyes on Anne Marie Peterson again. It had been over forty-five years. He made both of them feel so comfortable, and Sharon liked him from their very first meeting.

Dr. Avery began, "Anne, your mother had a hard time dealing with your condition at first, and that was to be expected, but she quickly readjusted her thinking and seemed to want the best options for you, but it didn't take long for him to realize that was just a farce to get him comfortable enough to release the two of you, "not that he could have kept you there. She seemed to have your best interest at heart at the time. Now I know it was all a ploy to throw me off, and when she didn't show up for your six-week checkup, I had a strong inclination that he had lost contact with you forever."

He asked Anne if he had seen any medical

professional since then, but unfortunately, Anne admitted to Dr. Avery that he hadn't. "Oh, my Lord, Anne. So, I'm going to venture to say that these have been some very miserable years for you. Would I be correct?" Anne lowered his eyes to the floor, and Sharon's eyes filled with tears she couldn't hold back.

He asked Anne how much Sharon knew about his condition, and Anne admitted that when things began to get serious between them, that's when he had no choice but to tell her the truth.

"Do you want children, Ms. Sharon?" he asked. Dr. Avery's question caught Sharon completely off guard. They had never had that conversation, not even girl talk around the office, but she quickly said no.

"Anne, quite frankly," Dr. Avery continued, "I am sure that you will never be able to have children, but how do you feel about having children?"

"The same way Sharon does, Dr. Avery," Anne responded. Hearing Sharon say she didn't want children made Anne know all the more that they were destined to be together.

Anne also knew that he should let Dr. Avery know that Sharon was a virgin. "Oh my," Dr. Avery said. "Ms. Sharon, may I ask your age?"

"Thirty, doctor."

Dr. Avery went on, "You're a rarity, young lady, especially in these times." Finally, Sharon suggested that she step out for a while and give Anne some privacy. "Thank you,

Ms. Sharon, and as soon as we are finished, I will have my receptionist bring you back in," Dr. Avery replied as his eyes followed her as she exited his office.

Dr. Avery was amazed at how large Anne's penis was, and he could now see why Anne would be worried about Sharon's virginity. In most of these cases, penises were much smaller. Sex in Anne's most passionate state could hurt her as well as cause her physical damage. He warned Anne that until he got him started on the right medication, there was to be no sex.

He told Anne that the male hormones in his body were the most predominant but asked him if he had ever seen any signs of vaginal bleeding. Anne quickly responded with a resounding no. "That's good, Anne," he said. "Even though your male hormones in your body are the most active, you still have one ovary on your left side," he explained.

Dr. Avery recognized what gender Anne was most comfortable with, but when he asked Anne to verify what he already knew, there was no doubt in Anne's mind that he considered himself a man, and that's what he should have been from the very beginning.

Dr. Avery proceeded to advise Anne that there wasn't much he could do for him physically after all these years, but he could medicate and closely monitor him. Pregnancy has not been an issue for Ms. Sharon until now, but he could not stress it enough how important it will be for her to get on some kind of birth control.

It wouldn't take much at all for Sharon to conceive if

everything was functioning in Anne's body the way Dr. Avery suspected it was. He cautioned Anne to be very careful because with the size of his penis and these intimate feelings that he has for Ms. Sharon, he needed to be patient, take it slowly and be very gentle when the time came.

He wanted to see Anne back in six months and immediately if any problems arose. When Dr. Avery finished examining Anne, Sharon was brought back into Dr. Avery's office. "Sharon, the two of you will make beautiful music together, I have no doubt," he said with a smile. "Love can hide a multitude of faults, but please be patient with each other because you both deserve so much. Just remember one thing, when love is there, it will find its way."

Dr. Avery continued, "As soon as you can Sharon, you must get on some kind of birth control. This is so important. I have already cautioned Anne that both of you are to be very careful and take it slowly." Sharon thanked him and assured him that she would be contacting her doctor as soon as she returned home.

They turned Anne's prescription into the pharmacy and waited for it to be ready. The sooner he started his medication, the better. They had a late return flight back that would not put them back into St. Louis until almost midnight, but it was worth the inconvenience to be able to sleep in their own beds.

So much had to be worked out before they could even contemplate having any kind of successful relationship. Neither of them was naïve in what they would be facing, but nothing would ever keep them apart.

They spent the night at Sharon's place for the first time in a while and what a wonderful change of environment it was. The feminine and masculine sides between each of them were so apparent. Even though Anne was living as a woman, there were many masculine characteristics in Anne's style of living.

That night, Sharon was restless and bothered. She straddled her sexy body on top of Anne and pressed her vagina against Anne's hard bulge. Anne could actually feel the heat from Sharon's body through her clothes. Anne thought it strange that when a man is in love with a woman, his imagination seems to work double time, at least his did. He had actually gotten good at knowing just what to do to put her to sleep, and he loved it. Watching her during an orgasm was the most exciting and moving thing to see.

The next morning as soon as Sharon got to her office, the first thing she did was call Dr. Lakeland and schedule an appointment. The receptionist tried to schedule her for the following week, but Sharon did not want to wait a whole week.

All of this was so new to her. Birth control used to be the last thing on her to do list, but her life had changed so much over the last few weeks. Having sex at thirty years old seemed so unreal to Sharon, yet so exciting. Just thinking about it made her wet.

By the time she got to Dr. Lakeland's office, she was filled with anxiety. "Getting you here used to be like pulling teeth," Dr. Lakeland said. "What's going on with you, Missy?" she asked and smiled.

Sharon thanked her for seeing her on such short notice. "Marie probably thought she was dealing with a nut case," Sharon said, embarrassed at the thought.

"Well, she did say you didn't sound like yourself," and smiled.

Marie and Dr. Lakeland have been in Sharon's life from the beginning of her teen years and were like family to Sharon.

"Sharon, honey, what's wrong?" she asked, sounding concerned.

"I just…"

"Just what, Sharon?"

"I just think it's time for me to be on birth control," Sharon awkwardly blurted out.

"Birth control? My Sharon?" Dr. Lakeland replied surprised. Dr. Lakeland guessed that this was the reason for the emergency visit. Dr. Lakeland was momentarily confused and questioned Sharon. "But you haven't been sexually active yet, have you, Sharon?"

"No, Dr. Lakeland." Sharon responded but Dr. Lakeland already knew that was something she wouldn't take lightly.

"Well, it's obvious you have met someone who's very special to you."

"Yes, I have, but there is no pressure from him at all.

Would you believe that the pressure is coming from his doctor? There's something going on inside the both of us letting us know that they both need to be prepared because neither of them wants children.

Dr. Lakeland knew that this was something Sharon was not taking lightly, and neither was she. Sharon valued herself as a person as well as her virginity and that was obvious.

"Sharon," Dr. Lakeland resumed, "I trust your judgment, but please keep in mind that pregnancy is not the only thing you need to worry about. Please be mindful of the other things as well." Sharon promised her that she would.

When Sharon left Dr. Lakeland's office, she felt like a woman ready to commit with no hesitation. She couldn't get home fast enough, Anne was waiting.

"Hi honey, I'm home. How was your day?" Sharon asked with excitement.

"Nothing short of perfect," Anne replied. He loved spending the day at Sharon's. Being there was like having her there. "I'm glad, Anne," she told him as she wrapped her arms around Anne's neck and kissed him.

Sharon smelled so fresh and clean. That's the only way Anne could think of to describe it. Maybe it was because he had never been this close and intimate with anyone before. Sharon had an intoxicating way about her that Anne would never get tired of.

"Dr. Lakeland called in my prescription today, and it

will be ready to pick up in about an hour," Sharon went on. All of this was scary for Anne. Just a few weeks ago, things were so different. Night terrors had almost taken Anne to the brink of insanity, but now that they had found each other, life had taken on a whole new meaning for both.

He was in such deep thought; it took Anne a while to realize Sharon had asked him a question. "Anne honey, where were you just then?" Sharon asked. Anne paused for a moment, and then replied, "Maybe your question should have been, where were you just then? I don't think you really want to know my answer to that," and he took Sharon in his arms and kissed her with a lust he knew he needed to keep under control.

Sharon could see it in his eyes, and she gently wiggled her way out of Anne's embrace. "I think you might be right," she said and suggested they go and pick up her prescription.

"Are you hungry?" Sharon inquired.

"Just a little, but I can cook for us if you'd like," he said. Sharon could get used to that because she hated to cook.

"That would be great, and whatever you fix will be fine with me."

Anne boasted, "Well, I make a mean chicken, bacon and spaghetti dish with fresh tomatoes, green peppers, scallions, and a homemade sauce that's to die for."

"Damn Anne, that sounds wicked," Sharon retorted.

"It is," Anne replied back.

Sharon pretty much had everything except the chicken and green onions, and by the time they went to the grocery store and got the rest of the items, the prescription would be ready, and she could start taking it that night.

They had so much fun together in the kitchen, and it made the perfect distraction from the obvious. Sharon did all the chopping, and Anne put everything together. "Anne, this dish is awesome. You're a wonderful cook, and I'll just bet you probably taught yourself."

"Yes, and you would be right," smiled Anne. He never followed a recipe. He envisioned foods as a perfect marriage that complemented each other, and when put together, the harmony of the combinations was an incredible fusion of flavor.

They sat in the living room around the coffee table on large throw pillows and ate by candlelight while soft music played in the background, setting the perfect mood. After dinner, they curled up on the sofa and talked about the week ahead and Anne's coming back to work.

"I'm ready to go back to work," Anne said. He missed her so much during the day when she was gone, even though he didn't see her much during the day, only when coming and going. Knowing she was right down the hall was comforting enough. It was already Thursday, and the week had gone by so fast. Regardless, they had accomplished so much.

After dinner, they lay there on the sofa together not wanting to move. They were enjoying the peace that had escaped them for so many years.

Finally, Anne gained the courage to talk to Sharon about something he had been dreading all week. There was no easy way of saying it. "When you come home tomorrow, I won't be here."

Sharon sat up so abruptly, it startled Anne.

"Why, Anne, is there something wrong?"

"Actually, there is, but not the way you are thinking. Tomorrow is Friday, and I am due back to work on Monday. I think we should spend the weekend apart. It's not something I want to do, and I believe you know that. I have not been back to my place since the Friday we went to Chicago, and I could get used to this arrangement quickly. You need your space."

Sharon knew he was right about spending the weekend apart, but as far as needing her space, that's the one thing she needed was space from him, and she told him so.

Sharon didn't know how yet, but they would have to figure out a way for them to be together permanently. She reminded Anne of what Dr. Avery said to them right before they left his office, "When love is there, it will find its way."

"Damn Sharon, our lives just keep getting more complicated by the minute, don't you think, honey?" Sharon pondered.

"Yes, but you know what? I wouldn't trade it for the world, and neither would you."

5

When Anne opened his eyes the next morning, Sharon was already gone. He missed her already, and the weekend hadn't even started yet. Anne got up and took a shower and actually looked at himself in the mirror. Memories of what his life had been like before Sharon came flooding back. The pain was still fresh, but somehow, he would have to get past it one day at a time.

He made the bed nicely just like Sharon did. He vacuumed and put everything in its place. He wanted to leave everything nice and neat like it was the first night he came. Anne spent most of the day there. It was peaceful and serene. Going back to his place would be hard after being there so much, but it had to be done, at least for now. Anne left about an hour before the time Sharon was to get home. This was going to be a long weekend.

Sharon arrived at work earlier than usual for a Monday morning. "Good morning, Sharon."

"Good morning, Chrystal."

"Isn't Anne due back today?" Chrystal asked, full of anticipation.

"Yes, she is," Sharon answered back. "You haven't heard anything different Chrystal, have you?" Sharon queried.

"No, I was just checking," replied Chrystal.

"I sure hope so. "I've missed her, haven't you, Sharon?"

"I know what you mean, Chrystal," as she headed down to her office. It really did seem like Anne had been gone forever and keeping things together would be strained to say the least, especially since they had not been together all weekend. Sharon busied herself trying to get a jump on things so she wouldn't feel so haggard when Anne did show up.

Today would be a wonderful surprise for Anne. Louise Russell from one of the lower buildings, Chrystal Johnson, and some of the other employees who worked closely with Anne on a regular basis had planned a surprise welcome back party for Anne. Of course, Sharon pretended not to know. They put up a banner that said, "Welcome Back Anne, We Missed You," with a card attached that everyone signed.

Someone brought donuts and a large coffee maker and lots of love. One of the staff was on watch for when Anne showed up in the parking lot, and when she entered the building, everyone yelled, "Welcome Back Anne, We Missed You." When Sharon heard all the excitement, she immediately went up front to see what was going on.

When she saw Anne and everyone gathered around, he looked so happy. Louise, from the other building, said, "Damn Anne, you look fantastic. You sure utilized those two weeks you've been gone." Anne just smiled and said, "Thanks Lou, I missed you too," and everyone laughed and made him feel comfortable.

Anne never wore dresses or makeup. He had on nice black casual fit slacks and a black dressy button-down shirt that fit his body to a tee. His short, naturally curly hair was cut to perfection and his skin looked like bittersweet chocolate against his beautiful white teeth - and oh, that sexy smile. Lou was definitely right.

"Thank you all so much," he said in his deep throaty voice.

"Hi Sharon. "Thank you for giving me the time off on such short notice. I'm glad to be back. I missed you guys."

"Anne, you look great," Sharon said, "And I'm glad to have you back as well. Now that you're back, we're going to work your ass off," Sharon joked. "Oh, before I forget, all of your work is still on your desk waiting for you." When she said that, everyone just about lost it. They laughed so hard. It was like being with family.

"Sharon, we finally pulled one over on you as well, didn't we?" Chrystal laughed. Sharon couldn't help but laugh as well.

"Chrystal, you are so right. It's not often you can pull

one over on me, but I was none the wiser, this time. I loved it."

You could tell how today was affecting Anne, and at last he remarked, "Well, I guess I'd better start earning my keep around here, but thank you all so much. There is nothing like being loved and needed." Sharon knew that last comment was directed especially to her, and it made her feel warm on the inside.

Anne thanked everyone again for their support while he was gone, then he headed to his office where he had always felt safe. He worked through his lunch break and still didn't leave until 5:00 p.m.

Sharon texted Anne at 4:45 p.m. "Leaving at 5:00 p.m."

"Your place or mine?" Anne asked in anticipation.

"Mine," Sharon texted back. "You always seem more comfortable there."

"Thank you for seeing that," Anne replied back. "See you soon."

Anne would have no problem getting into Sharon's place since she had given him a key.

"Today was so nice," Anne thought to himself and smiled. Life finally made sense to him. For so long, it hadn't, and he contemplated ending it many times, but today everyone was immensely loving. They weren't just coworkers, but rather, real friends, like family, and it felt so good.

The weekend away from Sharon was miserable. Seeing her today at least made it tolerable, and Anne realized he would never be able to be away from Sharon like that again, no matter the sacrifice.

Sharon left a little after 5:00 p.m. Anne's car was already gone, and when she pulled up in the drive, Anne was waiting. Sharon knew they had so much to talk about and being separated was at the top of their list.

When Sharon walked through the door, the first thing they said, almost at the same time was, "We can't do this again. Being separated was misery."

"Anne, when I saw you this morning, you looked very different," Sharon said. "So sexy, like eye candy." Anne couldn't help but enjoy the compliment.

Men never admit to blushing, but in fact they do, Sharon mused and smiled. Sharon told Anne she could see why Louise said he looked fantastic because he did.

Anne sat down on the sofa knowing Sharon would come and curl up on his lap because she always did.

"Anne let's take a shower together," and when Sharon kissed him, Anne almost came unhinged and instantly knew this situation was going all the way south.

"Sharon honey, "Listen…," but of course, she was not listening.

She stood up and took Anne's hand and led him to her room. She turned on the lights, took off all of her clothes and laid down on the bed. Just looking at her made Anne feel like he would lose everything pent up inside him.

Anne had never seen anyone so perfect in his life. Her breasts looked like they were made just for her body, perfect just like she was. Her nipples looked like forbidden fruit.

"Come and make love to me, Anne," and when she put her soft hands down inside Anne's pants and stroked his penis, it felt like every blood vessel in it was about to rupture.

He had never had anyone touch him like that before, and he lost all control. Her hands were so soft, yet so controlling, almost demanding him to respond to her touch.

It wasn't until Sharon encompassed his penis in her hand that she realized just how large it was, and she felt her vaginal walls constrict, but she longed to feel it inside her. She opened her legs wide. "Come and take me, Anne." Looking at that beautiful place on her body was like a secret place he had only imagined.

Her body felt like a hot oven, and the minute he tried to enter her, he knew he was too hard. Even though she was wet with excitement, she let out this horrible scream. She was driving him crazy.

The head of his penis was nowhere in yet, but he could feel her vagina attempt to grab it like a vacuum attempting to draw him inside her. What the hell was happening to them? The pleasure was like nothing either of them had ever felt, and Sharon's body just kept pitching upward. Anne tried desperately to control his thrust, but the pleasure was too intense.

She wrapped her hot thighs around his back. He knew he needed to stop, but both were in a trance. Sharon's eyes were wide open and so were Anne's, feeding off each other's pleasure.

Neither of them had ever experienced anything like this, and that's what made it so dangerous.

Each time it slipped a little deeper, Sharon would scream out in pain and pleasure, and she arched her back even more.

Anne knew he was hurting her. Why couldn't he stop? Had they gone too far, risked too much already? Suddenly, Anne felt something deep inside him that he couldn't even describe, but oh so dangerous. At the very last second, he pulled out and Sharon's whole body went limp. +

Anne immediately saw semen and blood on the sheets. All Anne could hear was Dr. Avery's voice in his head warning him, "Be careful, Anne. Be very careful." What had he done?

He immediately got cool towels and wiped Sharon's vaginal area. Nothing so perfect should ever have been tampered with. Sharon was weak and still out of it, and Anne was so overcome with sorrow; he couldn't hold back the tears that burned his eyes.

Sharon's beautiful hair was wet with perspiration, and when she tried to speak, he could hardly hear her above a whisper. "Anne, please don't be upset with me," she managed to say. Sharon knew she should never have pushed things this far when she knew they weren't ready, but it was time. It was time for her to be a woman and for him to be the man he was meant to be, but Anne could not help but blame himself.

Sharon loved Anne so much, and it hurt her to see Anne feel the way he did about something that was beyond his control.

"How could I not have been better prepared for this, Sharon? A real man would have. I should have used protection," he said. The feeling of him being inadequate upset Sharon because she believed it was more her fault than Anne's. She knew she had not been on her birth control long enough for it to be effective.

Anne knew he had made Sharon climax, and he knew he had pulled out, but was it soon enough? "I promise, I will call Dr. Lakeland first thing in the morning, and I will tell her everything that happened," Sharon said. Anne remained quiet.

If he had hurt Sharon in any way, he would never forgive himself. Neither of them slept the rest of the night, and the next morning Sharon called Dr. Lakeland as soon as her office opened. Dr. Lakeland said she could be a walk-in, and Anne went to work.

6

Anne's day was just the opposite from the day before. He entered the building without being seen, and that was a good thing. He had become good at it these past few weeks. He didn't feel up to any idle chatter first thing in the morning, and he hoped Sharon wouldn't take forever to let him know something or he might lose it.

"Good morning, Dr. Lakeland, I'm back."

"I see. "Am I not going to be happy, Sharon?"

"Probably not," because she wasn't happy with herself either, blinking back the tears.

"Well first, let me examine you," she said, and she warned her that it was not going to be pleasant. She tried to be as gentle as she could, but having a vaginal exam after having sex was like getting kicked in the same spot twice.

After Dr. Lakeland finished, she said, "Well Sharon, I can tell that your partner's penis is not small. Would I be correct in that assumption?"

"Not small at all, doctor."

"I can also tell that your partner used a lot of restraint."

"Yes, he did Dr. Lakeland, and he pulled out as soon as I reached orgasm, but he is terribly worried because I have not been on my birth control long enough for it to be effective."

"When did this happen, Sharon?"

"Just last night."

"Good. There is a pill I can give you called the morning after pill in case something unplanned happened. It will protect you."

"Oh, thank goodness," Sharon sighed in relief. The doctor knew Sharon was relieved, but she had to ask, "Sharon, if I were to guess that it was you who initiated this encounter, would I be guessing right?"

"No comment, Dr. Lakeland," she replied with tears in her eyes.

Dr. Lakeland could see how this was affecting Sharon physically and emotionally, and it distressed her to see her this way.

"Sharon, even though I have yet to meet this man who has stolen your heart, "she said," I know without even meeting him that he loves and respects your body with everything in him and is willing to sacrifice everything to nurture this relationship with you. Even though you have some bleeding, which is normal, there is no lasting harm."

"Oh, Dr. Lakeland, he will be so relieved." She couldn't wait to tell him.

She told Sharon to stay off her feet for the rest of the day, and she could return to her regular routine beginning the next day. "Here," she said. "Take this pill before you leave here." She gave her a cup of water, "And a warning "Sharon, no sex."

Sharon promised her that she would listen this time and apologized for being so reckless. "Sharon don't be. All of this is so new to the both of you, especially when love is involved. Call me anytime. I will always be here for you."

When Sharon exited through the reception area, she stopped at Marie's desk and whispered, "I love you." Marie touched her hand.

As soon as Sharon got to her car, she texted Anne. "The doctor put me on bed rest for the rest of the day. See you after work, honey? Please, Anne?"

Anne drew in a deep breath and released it with a sigh and texted back. "Alright."

"Please don't worry, Anne. I promise everything is going to be fine. If you can sneak away early, please do," she said, "But be discreet, especially with me calling in sick today. Having you in my life finally completes me, Anne.

See you soon."

By 4:00 p.m., Anne couldn't stand it any longer. He was so worried about Sharon and continuing to think about her kept him from being able to concentrate. All he could do was hope that no one missed him the last hour. He worked through his lunch break, so everything should be okay.

Anne made a quick stop at the florist and bought a single red rose and a card. When he let himself in and checked on her, Sharon was sleeping. She had on one of the prettiest nighties. She looked innocent and vulnerable, and knowing that he was the reason for all of her pain disturbed him. As much as Anne hated to admit it, maybe them moving in together was not a good idea after all, at least not now anyway.

While Sharon was sleeping, Anne decided to make homemade cream of potato soup with scallions, celery, real butter, and real cream. Anne hated generic and boxed foods. People fail to realize that with a little extra time and a few extra steps, homemade is just as easy, not to mention, rewarding.

The soup would be ideal on a cool fall evening. Whenever Anne felt overwhelmed or stressed, spending time in the kitchen creating something from scratch was a reprieve from dwelling on something he had no control over, at least for a little while.

When everything was finished, Anne went to see if Sharon was ready to wake up. When he turned on the bedside lamp, she was already awake. "Hi honey. It was so quiet I didn't know you were here yet," Sharon spoke softly, and Anne could see the relief in Sharon's eyes.

Sharon was so beautiful. She had a natural beauty that most women would envy, and her type of beauty is the kind that drives men insane. "Are you okay, Anne?" she asked quietly. Anne couldn't resist leaning over and kissing her lightly on the lips. Anne sat the tray on the bed beside her, and her eyes lit up like it was her birthday when she saw the rose and the card.

"We belong together, don't we?" she asked. The way Anne looked at Sharon made him want to push away all her doubts and fears.

"Taste the soup while it's still hot," he said without acknowledging he felt the same way. He couldn't imagine being anywhere else.

The minute Sharon tasted the soup, she knew. "Oh, my goodness, Anne, this soup was made from scratch." Sharon hated to cook, but she swore she could make a damn good food connoisseur. "This is fabulous on a cool evening," and Anne agreed. "When did you find the time to make this?" she asked.

"While you were sleeping."

Anne was happy Sharon liked the soup, but she didn't know what excited her the most, the rose and the card, or the soup.

"Anne, I think you missed your calling," she said. "This soup is what you would find in some of the finer restaurants." Sharon finished off the soup and asked for seconds.

Anne concluded that the soup won hands down over the rose and the card, and he couldn't help but smile.

"Come and lay beside me, Anne," and she promised him she only wanted to talk. "Don't you want to know what Dr. Lakeland said today?" she asked.

"Dr. Lakeland said she could tell without even meeting you that you love and respect me and my body very much. She also said that she could tell that you used a lot of restraint to keep from causing me any physical harm. Even though there was some vaginal bleeding, it was not serious."

Sharon could tell how much Anne needed to hear that. Sharon also told Anne about the morning after pill and how it can deter any chance of pregnancy if given shortly after an unplanned sexual encounter.

Anne buried her face in Sharon's lap and breathed a sigh of relief. Sharon could feel Anne's hot breath through her nightgown, and the sensation made her body flush. She gently stroked the back of Anne's hair and said softly, "Dr. Lakeland made me promise no sex."

"Dr. Lakeland seemed to know it was me who initiated what happened last night, honey, and I admitted it." Anne knew that as much as she hated to, she needed to use this opportunity to talk to Sharon about his feelings, at least until they were better able to control their desires.

"Sharon, don't you think we should hold off for a

while before moving in together, at least until we can get a handle on our emotions? Both of us are so vulnerable right now."

Sharon's words choked her as she asked, "Anne, have you changed your mind because of last night? Please don't use that against me."

Anne realized that this conversation was stinging Sharon, and he couldn't bear it. "Damn it, Sharon. You know that's not what I want any more than you do, and I feel helpless as to what to do. I'm not the same when we are apart, but the way I felt last night when I made love to you was like nothing I have ever experienced before. It left me overwhelmed with desire."

All at once, Sharon jumped up out of the bed, and said, "Let's get out of here for a while. Do you feel up to it?"

"Sure honey, I'll drive," Anne replied.

Sharon got dressed in sweats, a T-shirt and a jacket, and they were out of there. "Let's go north, it's really beautiful out that way this time of year," Sharon exclaimed with excitement. She told Anne that she liked looking at all the wildflowers because it always helped her focus and think more clearly.

"I used to drive out this way and take pictures. It's a photographer's dream," and she was right. This is just what they needed.

Sharon wanted to show Anne something, and Sharon was super excited about it. She had Anne turn on a road that led up to one of the most beautiful cottages Anne had ever seen. It sat back far enough from the highway that no one would ever have known it was there if they hadn't been looking for it.

"We'd better turn around," Anne said. "This looks like someone's private property."

"Not yet Anne, don't you just love this place?"

"Yes, it's beautiful Sharon, but we don't want to get into trouble for trespassing." Sharon got out of the car.

"Wouldn't you like to look inside, Anne? I have a key," she said.

"You have a key to this place?"

"Yes. It belongs to me."

"What?" Anne exclaimed.

"Yes. When I was eighteen years old, my mother's best friend, whom she called Nanna, gave it to me."

Anne couldn't believe what he was hearing.

"My Nanna and my mother were like sisters. Nanna never had children, and when my parents died in a boating accident, Nanna gave me the key and told me that whenever I needed to get away, I would always have this place to come to. Would you like to go inside?"

Anne almost couldn't speak. "Yes, Sharon, I'd love to." The minute they walked through those doors, they knew.

They had finally found their Haven.

The cottage had two bedrooms. The master bedroom was very large with a fabulous bathroom that had a wonderful walk-in shower. The kitchen was a chef's dream.

There was a large front porch with a porch swing, and in the back of the cottage, there were grape vines, a strawberry patch, and a fishpond fully stocked. Anne thought he had to be dreaming.

"When my parents died," Sharon continued, "This was the only place I could find peace. I was so lost and very unprepared for this scary thing called life. There were times I no longer wanted to live." Anne could definitely relate to that.

"I always wanted to live out here, but Nanna didn't want me living out here alone. She's getting up in age, and I really didn't want to put that kind of worry on her. Nanna always reminds me that this place belongs to me, free and clear, and when I find my true love, it will belong to both of us."

Anne had never seen a place so impeccable. Sharon told Anne that she had not been to the cottage for over a year until that first week he was gone. "I was so scared, Anne, and I didn't know what was happening to me. I felt this tremendous loss when you left."

"That day when she called and left that distraught message on your phone, that's how I felt Anne, desperate. I left work that day and came out to Haven House and fell asleep from exhaustion. I didn't know how I would make it through another week without you."

"That's why I told you today that you complete me, because you do."

Anne realized what a terrible mistake he had made when he heard Sharon's voice that day, and just how much he had hurt her. Anne knew at that moment he would never be able to live without Sharon in his life.

They sat down on the mattress that was lying in the middle of the living room floor, trying to make some sense of all that was happening to them.

Sharon had never put any furniture inside, only a mattress and something to cover herself. Anne asked Sharon how she managed to keep this place in such good condition, and she told Anne she has a caretaker who comes out and does the things that needed to be done, but Nanna promised her that she would never sell. Nanna told her that she was the only one who could do that, and she could never bring herself to. "I love this place so much, Anne."

Sharon was almost overcome by all the emotions that were going on inside her all at once.

Finally, she said, "I know it needs more, but more than anything else, it needs love. Nanna will be seventy-four years old in a few months, and I want to see her at peace and not have to worry about me and the cottage."

"I talked to Nanna about you, Anne. Nothing specific. Nanna knows that I have never trusted anyone enough to bring out here before, and it made her so happy.

Do you know what she said, Anne?" She said that she knew you were someone special because she could see it in my eyes, so she knew in her heart that everything was going to be fine.

"Anne, will you please come with me to meet Nanna? No commitment or anything like that. I just want Nanna to feel like she doesn't have to worry about me anymore living out here alone."

"You wouldn't have to stay if you didn't want to, Anne. Please come with me and meet Nanna."

"Of course, I will," Anne told Sharon. Anne could feel how much this place meant to Sharon, and he could definitely see why.

"Do you love me, Anne?"

"Damn it, Sharon, you know that without asking."

"Then nothing else matters," Sharon resolutely replied.

7

It was late when they got back to Sharon's place, and they both were asleep almost instantly. Anne was up and out early, which wasn't out of the norm for him, but also because Sharon had called in sick the day before and gave Anne the chance to get the jump on things.

Anne even managed to beat Chrystal in this morning, and he was glad. That gave Anne plenty of time to get his head together before everyone else showed up.

When Sharon showed up, she heard Louise Russell and Chrystal, the receptionist, talking up front. "Do you think Anne seems different since being back?" Chrystal questioned.

"Different? How exactly, Chrystal?" Louise asked.

Sharon immediately made her presence known. "Good morning, ladies," Sharon said, they acknowledged her presence. "Good morning, Sharon," Louise responded back, but Chrystal just continued where she left off. "Oh, I don't know. She seems maybe more preoccupied, like she has a lot on her mind."

Sharon listened intently without any input.

"It's just something I can't quite put my finger on," Chrystal commented further, really pushing the issue. "She even looks different. Nothing negative or anything like that, but different in a good way."

Sharon knew it was time to nip this conversation in the bud. "Perhaps she is more confident about herself, Chrystal." Sharon then attempted to change the subject.

"Hey Lou, I hear you guys have been having some real drama going down in your building these last couple of days," she interjected, trying to distract from the previous conversation.

"Girl, yes." Louise acknowledged. "There's been a strange woman lurking around down there, looking for someone, but not saying who exactly. She keeps insinuating that this person is not what everyone thinks, and she's talking about a lot of weird shit. Yesterday, she was removed by security and escorted off the grounds. Security told her if they caught her back out here again, she would be arrested, but something tells me this is not the last we will see of her. Someone said that she was seen wandering around in one of the upper buildings a couple of weeks ago."

"Man, this place really needs to up their security," Chrystal chimed in, and went right back to her previous conversation about Anne.

"Sharon, you and Anne used to be really close. Have you noticed anything different about her since she's been back?" Chrystal continued. "I know Anne didn't give you advance notice before she up and turned in her leave of absence, which is definitely out of the norm for Anne." Chrystal was definitely on a roll this morning.

Sharon tried not to lose her cool, but she'd had just about enough of Chrystal's shit, and she most surely didn't appreciate what she was hinting at either. Sharon explained, "Well ladies, all I can say is whether you are aware of it or not, Anne could have easily taken over three months if she had wanted to and still had time on the books with pay. So, maybe we should be counting our blessings, instead of speculating, don't you think?"

Chrystal almost choked, "Ninety days? Damn."

"Now, that's enough of the office gossip for today. Time to start earning our keep as Anne likes to say. See you later, Louise."

When Sharon finally got to her office and closed the door, she was visibly shaken. She didn't care for the way that conversation was going. She knew eventually she would have to mention it to Anne, but not until she figured out where Chrystal's head was at.

By the end of the day, Sharon's head pounded so badly, all she wanted to do was go home and be with Anne. They had plans, and she was not about to let anything spoil it.

About ten minutes before 5:00 p.m., someone was

knocking on her door. "Please, just go away," she said under her breath.

"Yes?" She responded, trying not to sound irritated. It was Louise Russell. "Hey Lou. I'm getting ready to get out of here, how about you?"

"Sharon, before you leave, I really need to talk to you about Anne."

Sharon could have sworn she felt steam coming up out of the back of her shirt. "Look, Lou, I've had just about enough of you and Chrystal earlier today." She could see that Lou got the message, but Lou persisted. She said, "Look Sharon, I love Anne about as much as you do. Maybe not in the same way you do, but I would kill a dead stump if it was trying to hurt Anne in any way." Oh boy, did Lou have her attention now.

It was as if Louise had knocked the wind out of Sharon's sails. "Yes, I'm listening."

"I know about Anne, and I've known for a long time, even before you ever came to work here, Sharon. Plus, I also know about Anne's mother. I am almost certain that the woman who's been lurking around here on the grounds is Anne's mother. She is out to destroy Anne, Sharon, and we cannot let that happen."

Sharon sat back in her chair and tears began to flow.

"Sharon, please don't cry. Just know that together we're going to fix this."

After Sharon gained her composure, Lou knew she had lifted a heavy weight from Sharon's shoulders. To be able to finally share with someone how much she loved Anne was like a healing for Sharon.

Lou told Sharon that she knew how the two of them felt about each other even before they could acknowledge it to themselves. "The kind of love the two of you have for each other is hard to hide," Lou said tenderly.

"You should be able to shout it from the rooftop, but you can't, not now anyway, and that is so sad. Especially when there are people like his mother out there just waiting to destroy him, and she will Sharon, to the point that he would never be the same again. I can see such a wonderful difference in him since the two of you came together, and we cannot let that change."

"How emotionally strong is Anne right now? she asked. "Not strong enough to deal with his mother." Sharon told Louise about the run in she had with Anne's mother a few weeks ago, and it was not pleasant.

"Anne is so intimidated by her Lou, and he hates it. She actually had the nerve to try to expose Anne's fears to me, because she thought I didn't know, and of course, I put her in check. I was sure I left her with a bitter taste in her mouth when she left that day."

"She has a way of making Anne feel less than Lou, and I don't like it. Lou, you just don't know what you have done for me today. You helped me feel a whole lot stronger for Anne," Sharon stated.

"Please Lou, let's talk again soon." "You know it, Sis. See you tomorrow," Lou replied as she walked out of Sharon's office.

After Louise left, Sharon could feel the wind in her sails again. Sharon had always felt that Lou had a soft spot in her heart for Anne, but she never realized to what extent. To truly know Anne is to love him. That's just the way he makes people feel.

Sharon crossed her arms on the edge of her desk and rested her head. "Please protect him from this cruel world," she ruminated.

Text: "Honey, are you ready to go? Send…

Text: "Yes, but I saw Lou coming out of your office. Is everything okay?" Send…

Text: "Everything is fine. See you when we get home." Send…

This day had been one for the books, but it was only the beginning because Sharon had no other choice but to tell Anne what was going on, and the sooner the better.

"Hi Anne. If your day was anything like mine," Sharon greeted.

"You mean hectic?" Anne questioned. "Exactly. "Sharon replied and they couldn't wait for this time of the day.

Anne admitted to having trouble getting back into the swing of things along with feeling kind of weird lately. "Weird how, honey?" Sharon asked.

Anne didn't know how to describe it exactly, but mostly he felt tired.

Sharon wondered if it could be the medication Dr. Avery had him on, and she reminded him that he wanted to know if he started having any problems. "Remember, honey?"

He wanted Sharon not to worry. "It will pass quickly. After I chill for a little while, I will be fine, Anne reassured her. Sharon gently suggested, "Anne, after you rest, could we go back out to Haven House?"

The biggest smile came on Anne's face. "Sharon, don't tell me you've named the cottage."

"Okay, then I won't tell you." She laughed so hard, she had to hurry up and go to the bathroom. "You almost made me wet myself, Anne," she said, still laughing.

"Well, whenever you're ready, I'm ready." They jumped into some old clothes and hit the road. "Honey, don't forget about our plans to go to Nanna's around noon on Saturday if that's still good for you."

"Sounds good to me," Anne replied.

"When we're done at Nanna's, can we come back and spend the day?" Anne smiled, but he was as hooked on Haven House as Sharon was.

Strange how Anne's tiredness suddenly went away. They drove in silence the rest of the way, taking in the beautiful scenery and enjoying life like neither of them had enjoyed it before.

They were so happy, and it wasn't fair that she would have to ruin it by telling him about what she had learned at the office today, but there would be no secrets between them, ever, especially something as serious as this.

When they pulled into the driveway leading to the cottage, they were like kids with a new toy. As soon as they got inside, out of the blue, Anne asked, "Now Sharon, what did Lou want today?"

The suddenness of Anne's question left Sharon unprepared. It disturbed her greatly that she had to spoil the mood, but this was too important.

"Anne, Lou knows about us, and she also knows about you."

Anne looked so shocked. "Did you tell her Sharon?"

"Now Anne, you know I would never do anything like that, and it hurts me for you to even think such a thing."

"I'm sorry, Sharon. I know you wouldn't, but the thought of someone knowing about me terrifies me." Anne exclaimed.

"Honey, Lou said she has known for a very long time, even before I ever came to work at The Company, and there is something else you need to know. Lou also knows about your mother."

"What?"

Sharon continued, "This all came about because there has been a strange woman lurking around on the grounds, wandering in and out of the buildings down there, and Lou is almost certain it's your mother. This woman has been escorted out of your building twice this week, and yesterday, she was escorted off of the grounds by security. They told her that if they caught her back on the grounds again, she would be arrested, but honey, Louise doesn't feel like that will deter her, and neither did she."

"Sharon had seen her in action, and agreed with Lou that she is out to destroy you, but we are not about to let that happen." Sharon emphatically elaborated.

Anne sat down in the corner of the room and locked his fingers behind his head. His locked fingers gripped so tight; it was obvious how strong a grip fear had on Anne. Sharon went over and sat down on the floor beside Anne and laid her head on his shoulder. Every muscle in Anne's body was rigid.

"Don't stop now, Sharon. What else did Lou say?"

"So far, she hasn't come right out and called you by name, but she has been saying a lot of crazy things." Sharon had to do something; she couldn't stand to see Anne suffering this way.

Sharon pleaded with Anne to please listen to what she had to say. "What your mother is doing is against the law Anne, and together we're going to make sure it comes back to haunt her."

Anne knew that Sharon had a lot of influence at The Company, and she also knew a lot of important people who would not tolerate what his mother was trying to do to him, not for one minute.

"Look at me, Anne," Sharon insisted. "Geraldine Peterson has hurt you enough, and if we are going to have any kind of life together, we will have to fight this demon together. Are you up to it, Anne?" Anne was visibly shaken, but he also knew that Sharon was a force to be reckoned with.

Anne took Sharon in his arms and clung to her so tightly it was like she was the lifeline to his salvation, and he knew she would never let him go.

They sat there holding each other, gaining strength. Finally, Sharon spoke, "You know what Anne? You may not have known this, but you have a true friend in Lou," she said, and Sharon laughed softly. "She said she would kill a 'dead stump' for you Anne if she thought it was out to hurt you in any way. She has always had your back."

Anne couldn't help but smile. "She actually said a 'dead stump', Sharon?" Then they both laughed.

8

"Good morning, Dr. Avery, this is Sharon Grayson." She reminded him of their last meeting a few weeks ago with Anne Marie. "Do you remember me?"

"Of course, Sharon," he could hardly forget her. "How are things going for Anne?" he asked.

"Not good, doctor. Anne's mother showed up here in St. Louis after all these years, and she has been coming out to our place of employment saying terrible things about Anne's physical condition. She has been referring to Anne as a Freak of nature and saying degrading things about him.

" So far, she has not come right out and called Anne by name doctor, but she will, and that will destroy everything Anne holds dear. I've asked Anne to press charges of slander against her."

"That's a good start Sharon, but who is your superior? Who is the person in charge where you two are employed?"

he asked.

"His name is Dr. Charles Robinson. Do you know him?"

"Sharon, the Gods are in your favor today," he gleefully retorted. "I am on several board committees with Charles, and yes, I know him very well. I'll just about bet that Charles is not aware that this is going on, is he?"

"Not yet, Dr. Avery," Sharon conceded.

"Sharon, let me get with Charles," he suggested. "This is what I want you to do. Before the end of the day, please have Anne go and file a complaint with law enforcement. It is imperative that he does that today, Sharon. Let them know what his mother is doing and file a restraining order against her. When she shows up out there again, she will be arrested. Remember Sharon, Anne must do it today so it will be in force next week when she shows up. This is very important."

Sharon couldn't thank him enough for his support.

"You are so welcome, Sharon. Geraldine Peterson has hurt Anne enough over the years, and even now, she is still trying to destroy her own child, but not while "he" was still breathing and had anything to do with it.

"Remember, I was there when Anne Marie was born. He didn't get a fair shake then, but he will this time. Talk to you soon and tell Anne to hold on tight. This is going to be a bumpy ride."

Now that Sharon had Dr. Avery's backing, she had plans of her own. She immediately told Anne everything that Dr. Avery told them to do, and by the end of the day, everything was in place.

That night, Sharon tried to get Anne to relax, but he had so much fear locked away inside him. He was like a caged animal, and she couldn't help but wonder how Anne ever survived his childhood.

Sharon was in deep thought when she heard Anne calling her name. It was likened to being awakened from a bad dream. Anne could perceive how much this was affecting Sharon as well, and he hated it.

"Sharon, you never cease to amaze me," Anne said.

"Why do you say that Anne?"

"Well, you care deeply about people, even to the point of giving them the benefit of any doubts you may have to the contrary until they cross you or someone you love, or even something you are passionate about. Then you can be dangerous as well. Not the violent kind of dangerous, but the devious kind. Yet, when I look at you now, all I can see is this sweetness and innocence that rocks my world."

Three months ago, there was no way he could have done this, but now that he had Sharon, he could do anything. "Having you in my life has made me stronger, strong enough to see this through. Thank you for loving me, Sharon. No one has ever loved me like this before."

Sharon was overcome with sorrow. She could not

imagine being in the world for forty-five years and never having anyone care about you.

Sharon wanted more than anything else to cure Anne of this cancer 'called a mother', and if it was the last thing she ever did in this world, she would.

They sat there quietly for a long time, not talking, just being in each other's presence. There was just one more thing Sharon wanted to do, and that was call Louise.

"Hey Lou, I hope I'm not calling too late," she said apologetically.

"Girl no, not at all. I've been watching a scary movie, and I'm as jumpy as a frog on a hot stove." Sharon laughed so hard and told Lou that she loved scary movies as well, the scarier, the better.

"Well, we'll have to get together one evening and rent some good ones," Lou retorted.

"That sounds like a plan, Lou."

"Lou, the reason I'm calling is to arrange for us to get together first thing Monday morning. I need to tell you what is going on so you can be in sync with everything. In order to pull this off, everything has to be in order," Sharon explained."

Louise assured her she was on board, and she would see her first thing on Monday morning. "I'll come down to your office and tell Anne I asked about him."

"Thanks, Lou, for everything," and she would make

sure to tell Anne what Lou had said. Anne smiled.

Monday morning arrived, and Sharon was on a mission. The first thing she wanted to do was talk to the head of security. He hadn't seen Geraldine back on the grounds since last week, but he was willing to bet that they hadn't seen the last of her. He let Sharon know that this time they would be ready for her. Thus far, Geraldine had not yet made it to Sharon's building. She was anticipating that hers would probably be next. Keith told her that Dr. Robinson wanted to be notified as soon as Geraldine showed up.

"Don't worry Sharon, we will be ready," Keith insisted.

Sharon was anxious. "Keith, when she does show up, would you please notify me as well?" she asked. "I'll keep my cell in my pocket on vibrate and wait for your communication."

"You know it, Sharon," he said. "Dr. Robinson told me to work with you and help you out in any way I can, so you don't have to worry. We will be on it."

"Thanks for everything, Keith," Sharon replied with a sense of relief.

Now it was all just a waiting game. Anne was very anxious and wasn't the same anymore. He was hoping that his mother had taken heed of the warnings and elected to stay away, but deep down in his soul, he knew she wouldn't.

Tuesday came and went, and there were no signs of Geraldine. Anne began to breathe a sigh of relief, but Sharon, being a good judge of people, knew Geraldine was just letting the dust settle. She would be back, and when she did, they would be waiting.

Sharon could not get Anne to go to Haven House all week, and they even missed going to Nanna's. Anne didn't seem to want to commit to anything anymore. No intimacy, no future plans, not anything. He wasn't behaving in a cold manner or anything like that. It was as if he was preparing for a loss if that makes any sense.

They were at the end of the week, and still no signs of Geraldine. Sharon hated what this was doing to them. She wouldn't allow herself to hate Geraldine because that would only be stooping to her level.

"Hello Ms. Pretty."

"Oh my God." Sharon gasped. It was Anne's mother. Sharon knew that voice anywhere.

Sharon felt her cell phone vibrate in her pocket, but she dared not touch it. Geraldine laughed. "It took me a while to find you," she said, sounding jubilant, "But it was only a matter of time," as she presented herself smugly.

Sharon had been waiting for this time as well, and she could be just as smug. "Find me, "I didn't realize I was hiding.

"How can I help you, Ms. Peterson?"

"Damn girl, you're sharp. You don't miss a step, do you? Well, you can start by telling me where that freak show daughter of mine is. You was hanging around with her the last time I saw you. I know she's around here somewhere, probably hiding under her desk."

Sharon was livid but kept her cool. "Ms. Peterson, I have no idea what you are talking about."

Geraldine persisted, "I'm talking about Anne Marie Peterson, one of your employees. I bet you don't know the truth about that He/She do you, Ms. Grayson?" as she snickered.

Suddenly, Sharon heard Anne's voice, "Mom, leave her alone and get out of here before I called security."

Geraldine laughed. "Call security, Anne. They already know about you. They know that you have been pretending to be something that you're not."

"Leave!" Anne shouted.

By then, everyone was out of their offices lingering in their doorways in a state of shock. "Listen up everybody. Y'all want to know what she really is? She's one of those freaks they call hermaphrodites."

"All right Ms. Peterson, that's enough." Unbeknownst to Geraldine, the head of security, St. Louis Law Enforcement, and last but not least, Dr. Charles Robinson, the CEO of Company, had been in Anne's office the whole time. They had heard everything they needed to hear in order to arrest her, but unfortunately, so had everyone else.

One of the officers said, "Ms. Peterson, you are under

arrest."

"For what? The truth?"

"Number one, failure to follow a direct order from security to not come back on this property. Number two, sexual harassment in a workplace. And number three, slander. Shall I continue, Ms. Peterson?"

When she attempted to leave on her own, they handcuffed her and placed her under arrest.

She looked at Sharon, smiled and said, "Well honey, at least you got balls."

"Get her out of here," Dr. Robinson ordered, barely able to control himself.

9

Had Anne's mother won after all? Anne's whole life had been exposed to everyone he worked so hard to keep the secret from. Geraldine had opened a wound that would never heal.

Sharon tried desperately to spot Anne, but she couldn't see him anywhere. After law enforcement left and took Geraldine to jail, company security returned to the building. It was quiet, and everyone seemed to be in a state of disbelief and shock. When Dr. Robinson saw some of the staff attempting to go back into their offices, he stopped them.

"No one is to leave the area until I finish what I have to say. I want hand-written statements from everyone present here today on my desk before leaving work today. I want you to state everything you observed and heard. Nothing that went on here today is to be discussed between any of you once you leave this building. Does everyone understand me?" he asked in no uncertain terms.

Everyone acknowledged that they did. He asked Sharon to please make sure Anne had some privacy for the rest of the day, and he would contact Dr. Avery himself.

"Yes, doctor, I will do it right away," she said, and her throat hurt when she attempted to speak.

Everyone was responsible for hand-delivering their own statements to him, and he would be looking them over before they clocked out. Dr. Robinson exclaimed for all to hear, "People, consider your statement a legal document." With that, once Dr. Robinson left the building, everyone went back to their offices and closed their doors. Sharon did the same.

Sharon waited until everyone cleared out, and then she texted Anne. All she wanted to do was get Anne away from there. "Honey, let's go home."

She waited for a response, but no reply came. Fear gripped Sharon's heart like a vice. What if, she mused. She couldn't get to Anne's office fast enough. She didn't knock or anything, she just opened the door, but Anne was not there.

Please, this could not be happening. Had she pushed Anne too far? Sharon felt helpless as to what to do.

Anne's mother was a vile and cruel person and had hurt Anne deeply. If she lost Anne behind this, life would have little meaning for her anymore, and then they all would lose. Sharon sat in her car and cried. Her whole body ached for Anne's embrace.

She couldn't go home if Anne wasn't there, and every

time she tried to call Anne's cell, it went directly to voicemail. "Please Anne, answer," she begged in her swirling mind.

Sharon had no memory from the time she left the parking lot until she pulled up in front of Haven House, and Anne was sitting on the porch, completely disoriented. It was as if instinct brought Anne to Haven House, just like it did her. It was so uncanny.

All Anne could say was, "I left my phone, Sharon. I left my phone."

Sharon was worried about Anne. There must be a limit to how much the heart can be broken, and had Anne's been damaged beyond repair? Today had been a nightmare, and Geraldine Peterson was what nightmares were made of. Sharon sat down on the porch beside Anne, and he buried his face in her lap, and wrapped his arms around her hips. She could feel Anne's hot breath through her dress. A shiver danced at the nape of her neck.

When Anne stood and picked her up in his arms and kissed her, she knew she would not be able to deter him this time. The desire was too great.

"Let me make love to you, Sharon. It's time." Sharon unlocked the door, and they went inside. Just the way he looked at her made her wet, and when he cupped her sex in his hand, he knew.

There was desperation in his eyes as he undressed her. "Don't be scared, Sharon. I won't ever let it hurt you. I promise."

The sunset streaming through the windows made Sharon's body glisten like honey and cinnamon. She was the most beautiful woman Anne had ever seen.

Sharon slowly unfastened Anne's shirt and slacks, and let her soft hands slide around the rim of his underwear. They were extremely tight hiding the huge bulge between his legs, and when she touched him, it throbbed beneath her hand, causing him to grasp her wrist.

She pressed her mouth against his and whispered, "Please don't hurt me, Anne. "I am so scared."

"Never would I do that," he whispered, but when her bare breast brushed against his chest, she felt it throb against her vagina.

She had never seen him naked before, and he was a masculine beauty, beyond anything she could ever have imagined. For his mother to call him a freak of nature was ludicrous. He had the most desirable man's body she had ever seen with a gentle sweet nature of a woman all in one person.

Even though the vagina was there, you would have to get up close and personal to see it. His penis definitely took center stage. Sharon wanted him so badly, but she gasped, "Please wait." He could hardly stand it himself, and he refused to penetrate her. "I won't Sharon, not yet."

Sharon got on top of him and tried to ease her hot sex down on his penis, and he grabbed her by her hips. He knew he was too hard, and he was not going to let it go deep. The pleasure of the way her vagina attempted to latch on to it and pull it inside her was like being sucked into a forbidden place.

He placed his hands on her hips and moved them around in a slow, smooth grind. The slow, smooth movement of their bodies together was like a hypnotic dance. Not too deep, but just deep enough. Neither of them could have ever imagined what pleasure being in love and making love to that person could be like, but the best part of all this was they were learning all about it together, for the very first time.

Sharon had never seen someone with such control over their own body. He could not only control his body, but Sharon's as well at the same time and bring the both of them to a musical climax at the very same time. They fell asleep, locked in one another's embrace, and now, they truly belonged to each other.

Early the next morning, they both woke up at the same time, and the real world was out there waiting to pounce. How they would survive in it was what they had to decide.

Anne asked Sharon if she would mind if he missed the day from work, and of course he should have known the answer to that, especially after what he had been through yesterday. When Anne told Sharon the reason, he wanted to miss work, it took Sharon completely by surprise.

"I am going to petition the court to change my name." No longer did he want Anne Marie Peterson to define who he wasn't any longer. "Will you help me, he asked?"

Sharon was stunned, but she said yes without hesitation. He didn't know what name, or any of the specifics. He only knew he was getting it done. He asked her if she could help him come up with an appropriate name for himself as soon as possible, and she was excited about it.

It was clear how much his mother had damaged him, but more than anything else, how she trapped him by making him live all of these years with a woman's name. She trapped him into something she knew he wasn't, and in the process, it kept him from moving forward or backward. A person's name is the beginning of their identity. What man would be named Anne Marie?

Anne was quiet, almost to the point of being subdued. Sharon still lay cradled in Anne's arms, and when she pressed her lips against his neck, it brought him back from a very dark place.

So many times, Anne wondered what kind of man he would be today if only his mother had taken him back to Dr. Avery like she led him to believe she would, like any loving mother would have done. Life would have been so much different, but instead, she chose to do just the opposite.

"Sharon, does my mother really hate my existence that much?" he asked, almost choking on the words.

Finally, he reluctantly released his embrace. "Forgive me, honey," he said. He did not want to make her late for work by listening to him hash over the past, and that's what it was now, all a part of the past. It was time for him to start a new chapter in a new life with her.

Sharon's heart was full. She headed to the shower, and he followed. He asked her where they were meeting today, and she said at Haven House with no hesitation. This was their home now, and the sooner they pulled it together, the better.

When he came home tonight with the paperwork and the instructions, he would have a new identity.

10

Sharon had to hurry. She had already showered, and all she had to do was stop at her old place and get dressed. She could still get to work on time. She didn't want to deviate from her old routine, especially after yesterday, and as soon as she got to her office, Lou came. "How's Anne, she asked?"

"Not ready to come back to work, that's for sure, but can you blame him?" Louise agreed.
Lou reminded Sharon that if there was anything she could do to make things easier for them to please just say it.

Sharon couldn't thank her enough. Her caring and kindness meant so much to them. Just knowing that she was backing them gave them so much comfort. It was hard for Sharon to put into words just how Lou's friendship affected her and Anne.

"You know, Lou," Sharon said, "I truly believe that

as long as we have one or two true friends, that's all that really matters. The rest are only acquaintances. Love you, girl."

"You too, Sharon. Call me anytime."

After Lou left, Sharon buried herself in her work the rest of the day to make the time go by faster because this was not where her heart was. It was wherever Andrew's was.

Andrew. Who in the world was Andrew? How did that name just pop in her head from out of nowhere? She got on the computer and looked up the name Andrew. It spoke, manly warrior, and that's when it came to her where she had heard that name. It was from her bible study group. They had talked about the twelve apostles chosen by Jesus, and Andrew was the first.

What a perfect name for Anne and why couldn't he have her last name, Grayson, Andrew Grayson She couldn't believe how perfectly it fit him, and she could call him Dru for short. Oh my God, it's the perfect name.

Sharon had a hard time focusing the rest of the day. Now she could see why Andrew missed her so much when he was off. The time just seemed to drag on, but even though her day was hectic, she felt rejuvenated. There was hardly enough time to get everything done, but she did her best work under pressure.

Anne's day was just as hectic, but he couldn't ever remember feeling such pleasure. There was hardly enough time to get everything accomplished before Sharon got home. The court documents were the easy part. He paid the filing fee, but until they came up with a name, everything was pretty much on hold. He could be John Doe as far as he was concerned. He didn't know why that made him laugh, but it did. He felt so liberated.

He knew when Sharon got home, they would work on it together, but right now he was desperately trying to get the new bed and the most wonderful bedding delivered to Haven House before Sharon got home. Sharon was the kind of woman who makes a man want to make the impossible possible. The furniture store promised to deliver by 4:00 p.m. if they could follow him out to Haven House. It was so secluded; he couldn't have given them the address even if he had wanted to because he only knew how to get there.

For the first time in Anne's life, he felt normal. By 5:00 p.m., the bed had been delivered and set up. Anne had picked up a bottle of wine earlier in the day and had everything he needed for a most magnificent dinner. He had never experienced this kind of joy before, and it scared him. Without Sharon's love and respect right now, where would he be? He quickly pushed that thought out of his head and concentrated on dinner.

They were having Jamaican jerk shrimp with fingerling potatoes and large beefsteak tomatoes. Anne was most certainly in his element in the kitchen at Haven House. Everything was ready, and he would grill the shrimp while Sharon got comfortable. When he looked at the time, it was almost dusk. It was a bit isolated this far out from the city, and he could see why Nanna would be concerned about Sharon living out here alone.

BOOK TITLE

"Anne honey, I'm home." At the sound of her voice, he breathed a sigh of relief. He had begun to worry, he had to confess. She wrapped her arms around Anne's neck and kissed him. His body fit so well against hers, and there was something about the way she smelled that drove him crazy. Damn, how he loved her. Sharon brushed her lips against his and whispered, "I love you, Andrew," and gave him a beautiful card. At first, it didn't register what she was saying.

Anne sat down on the mattress that was still lying in the middle of the living room floor, and Sharon sat down beside him. He slowly opened the card. "Welcome to my world, Andrew Grayson." She told him that the name Andrew was Greek meaning manly warrior, and how he was the first apostle chosen by Jesus. "If you take my last name Andrew, then I won't have to change mine when you marry me. Would you marry me, Andrew?"

Andrew couldn't believe what he was reading. He couldn't believe he could love her any more than he did already, but every day it grew stronger and stronger. "If you would have me, Sharon," he responded with his voice cracking. "I would be honored to be your husband."

Mr. And Mrs. Andrew Grayson. Now they truly complimented each other. So much had been missing from their lives until they came together as one, like two lost souls, wandering aimlessly through their daily lives. Now together, their lives truly had meaning.

"Dru, what is that wonderful smell coming from the kitchen?" Sharon asked.

"Dinner, but first, I have a wedding gift for you as well. Close your eyes, and no peeking," he said, "Or no dinner." He took her by the hand and helped her to stand and led her into the bedroom, making sure she was not cheating. The bedroom was more beautiful than he realized. "Now, you can open them."

Sharon opened her eyes. "Oh wow, Andrew. How in the world, Dru? When did you…?" She couldn't believe what she was seeing. It was the most beautiful bed she had ever seen. They held hands and went over and laid together. The duvet cover was like laying on a cloud.

It was apparent where the feminine and the masculine sides of Andrew came together, creating the very best of two people in one beautiful body and soul.

They laid there together like that for the longest time not even wanting to move. Finally, he heard Sharon say quietly to herself, "Thank you, God for sharing your love with us." Andrew thought to himself that he could not have said it better.

Dru went into the kitchen and poured two glasses of wine, bringing them back to the bedroom. "Get comfortable and relax, honey. Dinner will be ready in no time."

All he had left to do was the shrimp. Bigger was always better and those were huge. The wine, the mellow music in the distance and the new bed was an intoxicating mixture, and when Sharon realized it, she was curled up in the middle of it, and Dru was brushing her hair back away from her face. "Wake up Mrs. Grayson, dinner is served."

The dinner was not too heavy, but absolutely full of flavor and very satisfying. Andrew had finally found peace but so had she. You could see it in everything he did, and he deserved it.

After dinner, they worked on the paperwork Dru brought home from the court. They took extra care to make sure everything was filled out correctly with no errors. When they got to the part for his new name, it seemed so right. He insisted on taking it back first thing in the morning before he came to work.

The only thing that bothered him was it would have to be submitted for public record, and after everything had been approved, he would have to apply for a new social security card and driver's license. He knew all of this would have to be turned in to The Company but It had to be done.

His mother had crippled him long enough. The next morning, he got to the courthouse as soon as it opened. He practically held his breath while the clerk looked over everything thoroughly.

When she looked at the name he had chosen, she told him he would be notified if there was any problem. He prayed that all went well because he liked his new name and had become accustomed to it already.

After he left the courthouse, he hoped he would be able to stop and talk with Dr. Robinson. He wanted to talk to him in person and let him know what his plans were. Having him in his corner would make this transition so much easier, and he was determined to have Sharon stay neutral through the process. He told her as much. He didn't want any of this affecting her position at The Company. It was past time for him to start taking responsibility for himself, and changing his name was at the top of the list.

Sleeping in their wedding bed was like a fairytale. Sharon remembered Andrew's kiss and telling her he was leaving, but that was about it. He had so much ground to cover. She wanted so much to help him, but she knew it was time for her to step back and let him do this by himself.

She laid there for a few more minutes, and then she had to force herself to get up. She could not take the chance of falling back to sleep and not being there when Dru arrived. She took a quick shower and left. She still had time to stop at her place and get dressed. They would have to make Haven House official over the weekend, and the first stop was Nanna's.

When Andrew got to his car, the first thing he did was call Dr. Robinson's office. It was still early, but his receptionist answered. "Dr. Robinson's office, may I help you?"

"Good morning, Carol, this is Anne Peterson. Is Dr. Robinson in?" he asked in anxious anticipation.

"Not yet, Anne," she said, "But he should be shortly. Can he call you back?"

"Yes, please," and he told her he would be in his office all day.

"I will have him call you as soon as he gets in," she

said, and he thanked her.

He wanted so badly for him to be in, and he was confident that he would call him back shortly. Dr. Robinson was not the type to leave a person hanging half the day before getting back, but still, he was very anxious.

Being back in his office felt strange and unsettling after all that had happened just a short time before. No longer did he find it the safe space he once did. He texted Sharon to let her know he was there. It took her a few minutes to text back, but she did shortly after. "Is everything okay?" she asked.

"Just waiting for Dr. Robinson to call me back," he said. "The sooner I can get past all of this, the better. Say a little prayer for me," he said.

"Always," she texted back, and she would be thinking about him every minute.

"Let's meet at your place first and load up the trunk," he texted. "Then we can go to my place," he continued. He didn't want her to feel rushed in the mornings. "If you think it is safe for us to sneak out early, just let me know, okay?"

"It can't come soon enough," she texted back, "And I will text you when I'm getting ready to leave."

Knowing that Sharon was close to him down the hall made things a little easier, but not much. He settled himself down and surprisingly accomplished a good amount of work. He definitely had enough on his desk to keep him busy.

When his cell rang, he hoped it was Dr, Robinson, and it was.

"Good morning, doctor."

"How are you, Anne?"

"I've been better," he said. "Dr. Robinson," he continued trying to control his voice, "If it would be okay with you, I would like to come up to your office and speak with you whenever it is convenient."

"That would be fine, Anne. Come on up whenever you are ready."

Anne thanked him. He didn't take time to text Sharon or anything because he wanted to get this over with as quickly as possible. When he walked into Dr. Robinson's office, his secretary greeted him warmly and told him Dr. Robinson was expecting him. Andrew took a deep breath trying to keep his voice from shaking, and then he knocked lightly on the door.

"Good morning, Anne, come and sit down," he said in his easy laid-back manner that made a person feel like you were his only priority rather than a distraction or an interruption. Anne immediately felt his apprehension ease.

"Dr. Robinson, the reason I wanted to talk to you today is to let you know that I have petitioned the court to change my name." "Sir," he said without taking a break, "I know you are aware of what I have been dealing with my entire life with my mother, and I have hated my life and everything it represented. She failed me as a parent, and after forty-five years, I know nothing of or about my father. How could she raise me all these years as something she knew I was not, and then use a birth defect to humiliate me in such a cruel and public way? Does she hate me that much, Dr. Robinson? Her own child?" He seemed to plead for understanding.

Anne suddenly realized that he was coming completely unglued and that was not intentions at all. He immediately apologized. "Please, forgive me Dr. Robinson," he said. "My only intention was to let you know why this decision was so important to me."

"Anne, you have nothing to be forgiven for or apologize for. Never lose sight of that."

Dr. Robinson stood and came over and sat down beside Anne. "What can I do to help?" he inquired.

"Dr. Robinson, if you would be willing to let personnel and the business office know what my plans are, that would make my transition so much easier for me to maneuver through."

Without hesitation, Dr. Robinson responded, "Anne, don't you worry about any of that. I will take care of everything in personnel. Monday, or whenever you receive your documents from the court, bring everything to me, and I will take care of the rest. All you need to do is to go to Social Security Administration and apply for a new social security card and a new driver's license."

Dr. Robinson was keenly aware of how overwhelming this ordeal had been for Anne, and he advised him that the less he said to his coworkers, the easier this adjustment would be. "You don't owe anyone any explanation, Anne." Finally, he said, "Anne, you have given this company twenty-seven years of loyal service, and you deserve no less from me. We value you Anne, and I hope you know that."

Anne stood up. "Thank you so much, Dr. Robinson," and when Dr. Robinson took his hand, he could literally feel the burden lift from his body.

"Anne, please tell Sharon I asked about her as well, and to keep up the good work."

"I will, doctor." Anne assured him it would mean a lot to Sharon.

"Thank you, Dr. Robinson, for everything."

As soon as Andrew got back to his office, tears blurred his eyes as he tried to text Sharon. "Dr. Robinson sends his regards to you honey, and he said to tell you to keep up the good work. Leaving at 4:00 p.m. See you at your place but take your time. I will get started before you get there. I love you, and I'll see you soon."

"Love you back," Sharon texted.

Sharon arrived shortly after Andrew got there, and it seemed so long since they had been together. She was sleeping so peacefully this morning that he didn't want to wake her, but tonight would be their first weekend together in their new home, and they couldn't wait.

"Hi honey. Things went well today," Andrew said with an aura of inner peace that clearly showed. "Dr. Robinson was very easy to talk to," he continued, "And he spoke so highly of you, honey. That's why I don't want any of this to affect you in any way. You've worked too hard to get to where you are, and for my mother or me to ruin it for you is something that cannot happen."

"Dru, you have worked hard as well, and I'm sure Dr. Robinson made you aware of that, too," Sharon responded.

"Yes, he did, and if I had any doubts before I went to see him, I didn't have any once I left his office today, and it felt really good. We are fortunate to be where we are at The Company and to have Dr. Robinson as a leader as well as our supporter," Andrew acknowledged.

They packed Dru's trunk with as much of Sharon's things as they could. When they finished at Sharon's place, they followed each other to his. He collected all the mail and put it in the car. After they packed up as much as they could from his place and made sure everything was secure, his neighbor spotted him.

"Hey, neighbor." She hadn't seen him for quite a while and asked, "Have you moved?" "Yes, I'm in the process," he said. The last thing he needed was to get tied up talking to her, he thought to himself.

"Damn, Anne, you look so different. Have you been working out or something? You look great," she went on.

"Thanks," he replied. "Sorry, I really can't talk now.

I'm in a bit of a rush," he said, "But when I come back for the rest of my stuff, I will come by and talk."

Sharon kept a low profile, and the neighbor lady never noticed her sitting in the car. Thank goodness for that. Their last stop was Nanna's. They still had plenty of daylight left, and this was their most important stop.

11

Andrew was surprised. Nanna didn't live very far at all from his place. He felt so anxious. In his opinion, no one was good enough for Sharon, and neither was he, but of course she would never think that and would be very upset if she knew he thought that way. The only thing he knew for sure was that he and Sharon would be spending the rest of their lives together.

When Sharon signaled to turn into the driveway, he knew they were there. It was a small home and comforting to look at from the outside. They held hands at the door. "Honey, don't be nervous," Sharon said." Nanna knows nothing about your life, nor will she care. All Nanna cares about is that we love each other and want to be together."

When she came to the door, her eyes lit up like a bright candle. "Well, hello. You guys come right on in. I had a feeling the two of you would show up today, and I was right. Welcome, both of you."

Sharon spoke right away. "Nanna, this is Andrew. Andrew, this is my Nanna." Nanna immediately stepped up and embraced him. "Nanna, I call him Dru for short," Sharon explained.

"Dru, welcome to our family," she said, and her smile warmed Andrew inside. It was obvious that Nanna was sincere. He felt an instant connection with her.

"Thank you, Nanna. I hope it's okay if I call you that," he said, and automatically knew it was.

"Only if I can call you Dru," she smiled, and they all laughed.

"Come, let's sit," she said, and she took them both by the hand. "Dru, I am absolutely thrilled that Sharon has finally found that perfect someone for her, and it shows by the way you look at her. Nanna's approval meant everything to Sharon and it warmed her heart.

"Nanna, we are moving into the cottage. We call it

Haven House. I hope you don't mind."

"Mind? Honey, I told you a long time ago that the cottage belongs to you. I must admit that name is well-suited for that house because that's what it has been for you for a very long time and Dru, I can tell that it will be for you as well."

Dru couldn't help but be amazed at the insight Nanna had and how perceptive she was.

Nanna had never been married or had any children, but the two of them had come a very long way together, and this moment in their lives was bittersweet. Nanna went on to say, "This is what I have wanted for you for such a very long time honey, and now you have found your warrior," she said and smiled. "Spend every moment you can together enjoying one another."

Sharon was elated. "Nanna, I love you so much," and she went over and hugged her tight

"Haven House is quite a distance, so I'm going to stick the deed in the mail, so you won't have to be rushed," Nanna stated. She embraced Andrew at the door and when she looked into his eyes, she could see the pain. She told him that now, finally, they had all found peace.

When they got back to their cars, both sat letting the joy flow through them. This feeling of complete contentment was incredibly new to them, and they never wanted it to end.

When they got home, it was 8:00 p.m. and already dark, but this had been the most rewarding day. Andrew gathered the mail, and they went inside. Tomorrow was Saturday, and they had the whole weekend to themselves. They could take their time making plans and putting things away the way they wanted. Everything was so right now that they were one.

Sharon was instantly asleep, and Dru was not far behind her. When he woke the next morning, it was 9:30 a.m., and Sharon was still sleeping like a baby. He curled up next to her and went through the mail. It didn't surprise him that he had gotten something from the court, and a date had been set for his mother's hearing. Perhaps that was a good thing. The sooner he got past all of that, the better.

Friday, April 12th at 8:00 a.m. was only two weeks away, but he was not going to spend one minute longer dwelling on it or letting it affect their happiness. He was not out for revenge against his mother or to make things miserable for her, he only wanted her out of his life forever.

His life had so much promise now, and he knew that Sharon would be right by his side. He posted the date on the calendar, and he would mention it to Sharon when she woke up. She was sleeping well, and he wanted her to rest for as long as she wanted to. He loved her so much.

He laid there for a few minutes. This would be the perfect opportunity for him to go by the jewelers and check on the ring he was having designed for Sharon's birthday. It was going to be a birthday present and wedding ring all in one.

Her birthday was coming up on May 7th. She was a

Taurus, the bull, and there were times she could definitely be a bull while giving the appearance of a sheep. He already knew her ring size by looking through some of her other jewelry. He left a note on the pillow on his side of the bed letting her know he was going back to pick up other stuff and to please call him as soon as she woke up.

"Be sure and call me, honey, and let me know if there is anything specific you want me to bring. Be back soon."

Andrew still couldn't wrap his head around how much their lives had changed since they finally acknowledged how they felt about each other. Now everything seemed important. There is nothing like experiencing new things with someone you love more than anything else in the world. Two mature adults experiencing their first sexual encounter together was like nothing you could ever imagine. There was no right or wrong way of doing it, you just let it happen.

Andrew's first stop was the jewelers. "Hello, may I help you?" the salesperson asked.

"Yes, is Mr. Webster here today? I want to check on a ring I'm having specially designed, and Mr. Webster is who helped me. My name is Anne Peterson." He almost said Andrew, but soon, it would be official.

"Yes, I'll get him for you," she said.

"Hi, Anne. Your timing is perfect. It is ready for your approval. Are you ready to see it?" he asked.

"Yes, please," Anne responded back excitedly to the point that his hands were shaking. When he showed it to Anne, it took his breath away. It was exactly how he envisioned it and wanted it to be.

"Do you like it, Anne?" he asked.

"Yes, Mr. Webster, I most definitely do. I couldn't have asked for more."

"Well, Anne, you have excellent taste!" he said. "The emerald cut chocolate diamond turned out beautifully, and the engraving in the band fit perfectly – 'Dru, Forever Your Warrior'.

Anne told him he couldn't have been more pleased with the outcome, and Mr. Webster thanked Anne for the opportunity to create such a beautiful lifetime treasure. Indeed, that's exactly what it was meant to represent.

That special moment he had played over and over in his head, ever since the night Sharon proposed to him. That's all he had thought about since then, and her ring had to be perfect. Anne left the jeweler in a daze. When he got to Sharon's house, he locked the ring inside the glove box of the car.

He decided to take as many of her things as possible. It would make it much easier for her to get dressed from Haven House and not have to rush in the mornings. He was glad he had taken her car because her trunk space was so much bigger.

He practically cleared out her whole bedroom. He

emptied out the drawers, finished up the closets and everything in the bathroom and headed back. The new furniture would fit beautifully and accommodate all of her things. He could always get the rest of his things on Monday.

Sharon was not your typical woman, and he loved every minute of getting to know everything about her. Thinking back now, he always had.

When Anne got back to Haven House, Dru headed to the bedroom singing, "Hey sleeping beauty, but she was nowhere to be found. He decided to check out back, and there she was, not dressed. When she spotted him, she was so excited.

"Dru honey, come look at dinner, fresh trout." There were four of the most beautiful trout he had ever seen, and she was a beautiful, nasty, sticky mess. Her feet, her nightgown, and her hair were a mess, but there was a glow about her that lit Dru up inside.

"Come see if you can top these," she boasted. Andrew had never been fishing in his life.

"Awe, come on wimp. I will even put the worm on for ya," she teased. "Just throw it out there and wait." Dru kicked off his shoes and waded out into the water a short distance. He didn't have to wait long. Suddenly, something just about snatched the pole right out of his hand.

"Reel him in Dru, you got one and he's a nice size. Hurry, Dru, before he gets away." Instead of reeling him in, Dru literally dragged the fish out of the water onto the grass. They both laughed so hard, they slipped and fell, and now they were both a nasty, stinking mess.

"Now that's dinner," he boasted. "Well, I guess," Sharon said, having to admit Dru's trout was a pretty good size. Now she would have to teach him how to clean them. They took them back to the cottage and put them in cold water. They would be wonderful for dinner on the grill this evening.

Sharon stripped down naked right in the middle of the kitchen floor and headed to the shower. "Come on stinky," she joked. "I promise, I won't look."

She might not look, he thought to himself, but he sure as hell was going to look at her. This woman was going to be the death of him. He was right behind her.

Their bedroom was ideal. It was the master with all the features = a large master bath with a huge whirlpool tub plus a walk-in shower with wonderful jets of water that caressed the body from all angles. "You wash my back, and I'll wash yours," she said. The perfumed soap she was using was intoxicating.

Dru rubbed her smooth body and his fingers gently glided across the nipples of her breast. "How about the front?" he whispered in her ear. She rubbed her soapy body against his, and he could feel her body become weak against his.

He used the flat part of his hand, never inserting a finger, and knew her body belonged to him. He held her securely around her waist with one arm and continued to rub her between her legs with the flat part of his hand until she surrendered. He held her that way until her orgasm was complete, and then he lifted her in his arms and carried her to their bed.

She nuzzled him in his neck and was left breathless. "You belong to me now, Sharon. Never forget that."

Andrew could not believe how connected he was to this woman. He knew this might seem strange to most men, but he wanted to give her the ultimate pleasure, but tamper with her body as little as possible. He was the first man she had ever given herself to, and that was just as precious to him as she was.

The rest of the evening was spent talking and making plans and not getting a lot done. They talked about his upcoming court date with his mother, but they did not dwell on it.

It was decided that Sharon would clean the fish, and he would cook the dinner. Even trade, he thought, but he was in awe at how skilled she was at her part. You could tell she had cleaned fish many times before, and it took no time for her to finish the job.

While he prepared dinner, Sharon attempted to put away some of her things, but with very little success. She spent most of the time in the kitchen with Dru, but tomorrow was a brand-new day.

Sharon suggested that tomorrow they go to his place and get as many of his things as possible, so they wouldn't have to stop at all on Monday. "What do you think, Dru? she asked. He agreed, but suggested they get an early start, so they would have the rest of the day free on Sunday.

They both had leases that ended in a couple of months, and they were not going to renew them. It was best that the sooner they cleared out and cleaned up, the sooner they could turn in their sixty-day notices of intent to vacate.

12

Things were pretty much back to normal at work considering, and Anne seemed to be going through a wonderful transformation. No one could quite figure it out, but they were not about to ask. They would only comment on how great he looked, and he did.

Anne made a trip down to Lou's building one day and peeked his head in her door and spoke. "You'd better not be napping girl," and then laughed in his low sultry voice. It made Louise feel good to see him doing so well.

"Good looking out friend," she replied, "And I hope your court date tomorrow will be short and sweet."

"Me too, Lou. me too," and he kept on down the hall finding his way back to his own building. No more demons and nightmares, not anymore.

The next morning, Andrew's court appointment was early because they had work after, and that made it even more hectic. Andrew woke up not himself and felt like a double-edged sword. Sharon did everything she could to take the pressure off the situation, and they talked very little. They went in the same car, and Sharon drove. When they reached the assigned courtroom, they had plenty of time to get seated and be in place before everything got started.

Anne's mother entered with her court-appointed attorney, and when Dru saw her, his whole body turned rigid. He gripped Sharon's hand so tightly it almost blocked off the circulation. She massaged the back of his hand with her other hand, and he released his grip, but only slightly. He finally realized he was hurting her and rubbed hers gently.

"Court is now in session. All rise," commanded the bailiff.

Andrew tried hard to relax his body, but he was

extremely tense. When the judge came out and took his seat, he told everyone to be seated and asked if all parties were present.

"Yes, your honor."

"Anne Marie Peterson, please come forward." Anne stood up and approached the judge's bench. Thank goodness he was allowed to sit at the table with his attorney, or he probably would have collapsed to the floor.

The judge said nothing and took his time reviewing the paperwork. Anne wondered if some of it included the statements that Dr. Robinson made everyone write and turn into him. If so, no wonder he said they could be considered legal documents.

"Geraldine Peterson, you have been charged with sexual harassment at your daughter's place of employment, along with slander, and returning to a private place of business after being escorted off by security. Is that correct?"

"Yes," was her response. Again, the judge said nothing and continued to examine more paperwork that was handed to him by the clerk.

"Anne Marie, it has also just been brought to my attention that you have petitioned this court to change your name. Is that also correct?"

Andrew's whole demeanor changed and seemed to come alive.

"Yes, your Honor, that is correct."

They could hear his mother saying something to her attorney. "Quiet, please," the judge said. Well, Andrew Grayson, we might as well not waste the court's time unnecessarily by setting another court date, so let's just kill two birds with one stone, shall we? Ms. Peterson, it seems that your *son* wishes you no undue stress or legal problems. He only wants to be free of the past that has haunted him all his life. He has only requested that you stay away from him and no longer come anywhere near him again. If you do Ms. Peterson, you will be in contempt of this court and will be held liable, and I will not hesitate to do just that. I assure you that I will not be as kind as Andrew has been."

He told her that he had Andrew's complete medical history in front of him, and that no child should have ever been made to endure what he has been through and still be tortured by you forty-five years later.

"Consider this a warning from this court, Ms. Peterson. Andrew Grayson is your new name. The court fully understands why you would want to change it, and this court has obliged."

Sharon stood up and when Andrew came back to his seat, she collapsed in his arms. Life had just begun for them, and it was bittersweet.

They couldn't get out of there fast enough, and when they got to work that morning, the first place they went was to share the good news with Louise. When she saw them, she knew things had gone well. She was so happy.

"Guys, we're going to have to get together and

celebrate," Lou said.

"We will and soon, Lou," Sharon assured her. The rest of the week went by fast. It was like they blinked, and it was Friday.

Right at 5:00 p.m., Sharon got a text from Andrew. "Running a little behind, but I will see you at Haven House. Get dinner started. Ha! Ha!

"Boy, he has really been on a roll lately," Sharon thought to herself. Her birthday was a week away, so she knew he was up to something, but she didn't know what. It was driving her crazy.

Two can play that game. She would have to show him that just because she did not like to cook, didn't mean she didn't know how to. It was time for her to show him a side of her that he knew nothing about.

"Don't underestimate me, bub," she murmured to herself. Nanna had taught her a few tricks in the kitchen, and it was time to spring it on him. "Hot fried chicken wings with homemade buttermilk waffles. I will have him licking his lips and begging for more, Mr. Smart Ass."

They desperately needed to start shopping for furniture. They didn't even have a dining room table. As soon as she got to Haven House, she went out into the shed and retrieved a card table and two chairs. She had the perfect tablecloth and napkins, and he was going to need them with this southern meal.

All she had to do was fry the chicken in her soulfully

seasoned cast iron skillet Nanna had given her and keep it warm in the oven. She made the batter for the waffles which would be made last and served with warm maple syrup or strawberry preserves. All he needed was a bib. She made homemade sweet tea with fresh lemons, and dinner was ready. She even picked up some ice-cold beer, just in case.

"Sharon honey, where are you?"

"Right here Dru, putting the finishing touches on dinner. Would you like a cold beer?"

"Damn, Sharon, that sounds great." He hadn't had a cold beer in a long time. "By the way, what are we having for dinner?"

"Fried chicken wings and homemade waffles."

"Sharon, you wouldn't lie to me, would you?" he said. She couldn't help but smile.

"Just relax, take your shoes off and get comfortable. I'll start the waffles while you enjoy your beer." When she took the fried chicken out of the oven and set it on the stove, he almost choked on his beer.

"I'll start the waffles. Just relax honey," she said nonchalantly, but she almost couldn't contain herself.

"Damn Sharon, that fried chicken smells wonderful."

"Thanks honey. I just needed to prove a point," she said.

"And what's that?"

"Well, no husband wants a wife who can't cook, so now you know I can, but I don't like to." He took her in his arms and kissed her, and the first thing she detected was the taste of fried chicken.

"You thief! Did you steal a piece of chicken while my back was turned?"

"I'm ready to eat when you are honey," he said with the biggest grin on his face. The evening was perfect. Andrew ate four chicken wings, and they weren't small ones by any means.

"Sharon, this little table for two is so intimate. Where did you get it?" he asked.

"I'm so glad you reminded me. We must go furniture shopping. I happened to remember having this card table out in storage. Thank goodness, or we would have been dining on the floor," and they both laughed.

"Honey, I totally love the furniture you picked for our bedroom. We will have to pick the right style for the living area, and the kitchen will be your department."

"Well, Sharon, the living room will be left up to you, but what are you going to do with the furniture at your place?" he questioned. He continued, "I love your furniture. Would you consider bringing it out to the cottage?"

Sharon got excited at that idea. "You wouldn't mind, Dru?"

"No, not at all. I love your place. The week I spent there before I came back to work was really where my healing began. I never wanted to go back to my place. We can donate the furniture from my place and then get everything cleaned and ready to turn in the keys. Time is getting close for us to turn in our written notices to our property management."

It was agreed that he would make some calls the next day and have someone pick up everything from his place while she arranged for a moving company to bring her furniture out to the cottage. They would begin tomorrow, and if they were lucky, they could have everything moved in by Friday. They went over and took inventory of everything at Sharon's place and made the necessary arrangements with the moving company for Thursday morning.

Andrew told her that he would hold down the fort for her at work while she attended to the moving. "Enjoy your day off, and remember, have them set things where you want them before they leave. I mean it, Sharon," Andrew insisted. That's what they are paid to do, not just sit things down and leave us with a mess."

She promised that she would. He would be home right after work, and they could get a lot done together.

Andrew donated his furniture to a safe house for abused women and their children. The shelter was so grateful. His furniture was nothing to balk at either. He had taken good care of it, and everything was working out smoothly. Soon, they would be able to relax and enjoy Haven House, just like Nanna said.

Sometimes, things seemed too good to be true, and that scared Sharon. She would never say it to Andrew, but there were times she would wake up in the middle of the night with the most unsettling feeling that would keep her awake for hours. She would snuggle down close to him and eventually manage to get back to sleep.

13

Sharon had a short week with a lot to do in four days. Dr. Robinson had given her a special assignment that he wanted only her to work on, and it would take her the rest of the week to finish it, but she loved the challenge. She did her best work under pressure. Having Dr. Robinson's mentorship is what propelled her up the ladder these last few years, and she knew he would not be disappointed this time.

Sharon has only been at The Company for six years, but she has done well. When she first came to The Company, she started out as an intern working directly under Dr. Robinson's supervision and guidance. Holistic medicine is his baby. Sharon's Nanna was how she came to meet him. They had been school friends, and she knew about The Company and his expertise in holistic medicine. That was the starting point of The Company's existence.

Holistic medicine's philosophy considers the whole person, and if one part is not working properly, every other part will be affected, and Sharon's emotional instability was completely out of control. When Nanna heard about Dr. Robinson taking interns into the program, she contacted him, and he was overjoyed to hear from her.

She shared with him about Sharon's parents being killed in a boating accident, and he recalled hearing about it, but would have never made the connection. That's how Sharon and Dr. Robinson's relationship began.

One year later, she became supervisor of the marketing department. This position was not given to her as a favor to her Nanna and her friendship with Dr. Robinson. Sharon legitimately earned it, and holistic medicine was truly where her healing began.

By Wednesday, she had everything completed, and Dr. Robinson's forthcoming acknowledgment of a job well done left Sharon feeling gratified. Now she only hoped everything would fit in their new home like she wanted it to. "Only time will tell," she thought to herself.

Dru texted. "They picked up everything today. Going to clean up. See you at home."

Sharon texted back. "With the two of us working together, we can be through sooner, and then our weekend will be free."

"Thank you, honey," Dru texted back. "See you soon."

It took no time to finish up at Dru's place. You could tell he was good at keeping things neat, and with it being only him, cleaning up was a breeze.

"Sharon, do you remember the night we slept on the floor at your place?" he reminisced. "You took those wonderful covers from your bed, and we camped out in between the sofa and the loveseat creating our own secret world." Sharon still found it hard to imagine what having her presence in his life meant to Dru. "Sometimes, just the thought of losing all of this scares me so badly that it keeps me awake at night," he confessed.

Sharon, listening to him, was like Deja Vu. It was weird that he was experiencing the same fears that kept her awake so many nights as well. It was mind-blowing how connected they were to each other.

She knew exactly what he meant. She had never shared this with anyone until now, but sometimes in the middle of the night she would feel threatened as well. They sat down on the floor together so close, almost like a safety net for the other, and for an extended period of time, they talked. It was as if there was no one else in the world but them.

"Maybe things are too perfect for us," he said. "Do you think that sometimes things can be too perfect, too right, Sharon?" She felt like something gripped her heart, and she felt physical pain.

"We deserve this Dru," she finally managed to speak, almost defiantly.

Now that they had finally become one, it was like she had always loved him. When she thinks back now, she had always viewed him differently from her, not like another woman at all. Strong, yet so gentle, touching her in ways she couldn't even put into words. Sharon truly believed that the day he saved her life was when it all became clear and absolute, and after that, she never wanted anyone else to touch her but him.

"We were meant to be together Dru, and nothing will ever be able to keep us apart." They stood up, and he took her in his arms, gently rocking her back and forth. They left without saying another word all the way to their new home, Haven House.

They were up and out the door early the next morning, and they didn't have time to dwell on anything else. Each of them was on a mission. Andrew wanted to get there early to cover for Sharon's absence, and Sharon wanted to be at her place before the movers arrived.

Her day seemed hectic, but by the end of the day, it would all be worth it. Everything was organized and ready to go, so things should go smoothly. By noon, the truck was packed and ready to leave. It was about a thirty-minute drive to Haven House, and by the time Andrew got home, everything was unloaded and in its place. It had been a very trying day, but worth it all. The movers were great. She couldn't have asked for better service, and when Dru got home, he was pleased as well.

"Honey, Dr. Robinson came down today looking for you," he said casually.

"Damn, the minute I miss a day, something like this always happens."

"Sharon honey, please settle down. Dru told him that something important had come up that you had to take care of and he didn't seem to have a problem with it at all Sharon. If there was a problem, he would have called you, don't you think?"

"Well, I guess," she said, still frustrated, "Just as long as there wasn't a problem with my assignment. That's the most important thing."

"In fact, he seemed very pleased today. Dr. Robinson said to tell you to enjoy your day off, and he would see you tomorrow."

"Dru, thank you for being there for me today," and she put her arms around his neck and kissed him.

Things had been so busy, Sharon suggested that since tomorrow was Friday, they should consider working through their lunch break and leave early. That sounded like a good plan to Dru.

The next morning, Sharon was up and dressed early. She kissed Dru and told him she was going in a little earlier today just in case Dr. Robinson wanted her to add some finishing touches to her project.

"Okay honey, see you soon. "Text me if you need me to do anything. Love you."

The day went by fast. She had only talked to Andrew once the entire day, and then, he was uncharacteristically abrupt with her. She had never known him to not have time to communicate with her, especially since they were trying to leave early. She had forgotten to remind him of that, and he hung up quickly. Oh well, she could text him a little before 4:00p and remind him. Since she hadn't heard from Dr. Robinson at all today either, she guessed that everything was fine, just like Andrew said. She waited until 4:30 and still she had not heard from Dru, so she decided to text him. "Honey, getting ready to leave. Are you ready?"

Her phone rang, but it was some last-minute stuff she could deal with on Monday. She checked her phone and still no text back from Dru. Things had seemed strange all day. In fact, she had not even talked to Lou today, which was odd. Finally, she went out to the lobby, and Dru's car was still in the parking lot. Well at least he wasn't gone. Maybe he just got tied up at the last minute. She decided to see if she could give him a hand to speed things up.

She knocked on the door, but no answer. Finally, she opened the door and peeked inside, and boy did she get the shock of her life. Nanna, Dr. Robinson, Dr. Avery, Louise, all of them, were in Dru's office. "Happy birthday!" They all shouted in unison. "It took you long enough," Lou said. Nanna came over and hugged her. Sharon was speechless. Dr. Robinson immediately spoke up. "I'm first, plus, I'm the boss." Everyone laughed so hard.

"Sharon, I want to let you know that your creative style and the attention to detail you put into the project I assigned you has put this company in the forefront along with other major companies in the country. It's all because of the pride you take in your work and the attention to every detail that you consistently give to your work that has proven you are a perfectionist and a true professional. We here at The Company value people like you, Andrew, Louise, and many others as well. I want to be the first to tell you that you have been officially promoted to Executive Administer for this entire building! Not just your department, but all departments starting today. No one deserves it more than you."

Shock was an understatement to describe what Sharon was feeling at that moment, especially because it was so unexpected.

"Oh, and before I forget," Dr. Robinson continued, "You do know that a great big bonus and raise goes along with this promotion."

Everyone applauded, and Sharon had to sit down. Her legs felt like jelly.

"Dr. Robinson, "you have no idea what this recognition means to me," she stammered, trying to gain her composure. "I love The Company and everything it stands for, so it shows through my work, but most of all, because of your mentoring, doctor. The day you accepted me into your program, you saw past the frightened young woman who was ill-equipped to face the realities of what she was truly capable of, but you did. For that, I can't find words adequate enough to express what this means to me. If my Nanna hadn't reached out to you, her old childhood friend, I would not be where I am today. Because of the two of you, I have been truly blessed." Dr. Robinson and Nanna were immediately at her side.

"We are not through with you yet, Sharon," and he laughed. Andrew also has something to say as well, and we all have been privileged to be invited."

It was quiet enough to hear and pin drop, and Dru was beyond nervous. He pulled up a chair right in front of Sharon and sat down. He took both of her hands in his. Their eyes fixed on each other.

"I love you, Sharon, with all that I am, and that's how you accepted me with no stipulations. So, I gave you my heart to put with yours, and together, we became one. " But take care for he was fragile and easily broken like fine China. If you look close, you can see the weaknesses, the chips, those ever-so faint hairline fractures, some of them beyond repair. But you gave me your love, and I gave you mine, and together we are strong. Love conquers all. No longer do I want to live life without having you a part of it Sharon, so would you honor me and please be my wife?"

Dru slipped one of the most beautiful rings on

Sharon's finger she had ever seen. Everyone in the room seemed under a spell, and Sharon's eyes never left his. "I love you, Andrew, my warrior. I've saved myself just for you because I knew we truly belonged together, even when we were afraid to admit it to ourselves or each other," and they smiled. "Andrew Grayson, I would be proud to be your wife."

The four people there today were the only ones privileged enough to share this most private moment with the two of them. They would have a private ceremony at Haven House soon, and the people present would sign as witnesses.

Dr. Avery's heart was full of joy. "When your plans are finalized, Sharon and Andrew, I would be proud to be present." He hugged Andrew tightly and left abruptly. Nanna was so happy. Before leaving, she pressed an envelope in both of their hands. "Open it when you get to Haven House," she said, the tears burning her eyes. It was the perfect ending to the most perfect day.

Before Louise left, she said, "Sharon, you just have to let me help pick out your dress." Sharon embraced her.

"Lou, I wouldn't have it any other way," and they cried tears of joy together.

"Sharon, your ring is beautiful. It fits just like the two of you," she continued. "I can tell it was designed just for you with love. God's blessing on both of you and your upcoming nuptials."

After everyone had left, Andrew took Sharon in his

arms. "Are you ready to go home, Mrs. Grayson?"

"I'm right behind you, Mr. Grayson."

14

The weekend was like a whirlwind. It came and went so fast. They decided to have the ceremony on Sharon's birthday, so that every year, they could celebrate both together. Sharon talked to Lou two or three times, and they made plans to go dress shopping on Monday after work because they didn't have much time to spare. Sharon's birthday was only a week away.

In just one more week, she would be Mrs. Andrew Grayson, and then there was her new position. She knew it would be a challenge, but with the two of them working together, it would be a breeze.

She looked at the hypnotic ring on her finger. It was breathtaking, and the engraving in the band said it all, 'Dru, Forever Your Warrior'. She could feel the love he put into every detail of the design of this ring.

Andrew's yelling brought her out of the wonderful daydream she was having. "Come on, Mrs. Grayson, we're going to be late." "I'm coming. I'll see you in the parking lot," she yelled back. They had always gone in separate cars; it looked more professional that way. They wanted to call as little attention to themselves as possible, and the fewer people that knew anything about them, the better.

Like she has always said, as long as they had one or two friends, that's all they ever needed, and they were blessed two-fold. The rest were only acquaintances. They both pulled up in the parking lot at the same time. Sharon stalled for a few seconds before getting out of her car. She needed a little extra time to pull herself together. Her head was still reeling from Friday.

Their eyes met, and they were lost in the moment. It was as if there was no one else in the whole world but them. No touching, that would not have been appropriate in the parking lot, but they were drawn to each other like magnets.

Neither of them realized that danger was near.

The day that Andrew was shot wasn't like a blur, not at all. It was right up in your face; reality. The look of shock in his eyes she would never forget. Sharon heard the first shot, but her entire focus was on Andrew. Then she saw her. It was Andrew's mother. Lou was getting out of her car and immediately called 911.

Sharon dropped to her knees beside him. "Dru honey, please open your eyes. Please. Dru, can you see me, honey? I'm here. A tear from Sharon's eye dropped on his face, and he opened his eyes briefly, looking into her very soul. Please don't leave me, Dru, please don't."

Sharon could hear the sirens off in the distance getting closer and closer, and she could feel someone trying to move her away, but all she wanted was to see life in her lover's eyes, and that would be enough. Helplessness and a most morbid feeling of emptiness overtook Sharon. "Sharon, standup right now." It was Louise. "We have to go." Sharon didn't know how she got into Louise's car, but now, she was stooping to Geraldine's level, and hate overcame her. She hated Geraldine with an intense passion, so much so, she became nauseated. Rage was boiling in her belly. Was this the same thing Geraldine was feeling when she did this hideous deed? Did she, could she, hate her own child so much as to even attempt to take life from him?

"She did not give Dru this life, Lou. How dare she attempt to take it away?" If Dru were to die, she would have taken two lives because she would never be alive inside again.

Before she realized it, they were in the Emergency Room parking area. Lou came around and opened the door and helped Sharon stand. She looked at Sharon and spoke. "She killed herself, Sharon. Geraldine Peterson is dead."

The bright lights in the Emergency Room were blinding, and she braced herself against the receptionist's desk. "Andrew Grayson, where is he?" Sharon's legs felt like they were made of stone, and she was hardly able to move them.

"Are you family?"

"Yes. "We're going to be husband and wife. "I'm Sharon Grayson." The receptionist looked at Sharon, bewildered. "Please, he needs me," Sharon begged.

Louise spoke. "Can we see him?"

"Not now, but soon," she responded.

Sharon dropped to her knees and rocked back and forth, almost incoherently. Louise and the nurse helped Sharon to stand and sat her down in a wheelchair. The nurse seemed concerned about Sharon's mental state. "I'm going to have someone come and take a look at her," she said.

"How dare Geraldine take the cowardly way out, Lou? She deserved to pay for what she did. How dare she, Lou?" Louise did everything she could to console Sharon, but she could tell Sharon was on the brink of snapping, and she feared for her emotional state if she didn't pull herself together.

"Sharon, we will get through this. I promise you that we will, but Sharon," Lou turned to Sharon and forced her to make eye contact, "You've got to keep it together for Dru. Right now, he's going to need your support now more than ever, and you must have a clear head."

Sharon gripped Louise's hand and held on tight. The nurse came back and took Sharon's blood pressure and checked her pupils. "Ms. Grayson, you must try to calm yourself," and she checked Sharon's knees when she dropped to the floor to make sure she had not injured herself.

Sharon took a deep breath. "How is he nurse?" her voice cracking.

"Not good, but Dr. Clarke is with him now."

"Sharon Grayson?"

Sharon was up out of the chair so fast; she almost lost her balance. The doctor approached her. "Ms. Grayson, please, sit back down, we will take you back shortly." Sharon's mental state was visibly fragile, and Dr. Clarke knew that. He knew he had to give her something to hold on to. "Dr. Clarke, please tell me Dru is going to be okay." He pulled up a chair in front of Sharon.

"Sharon, listen to me," he said quietly. He was not going to lie to her. "Andrew's injuries are critical, and I'm going to need your help, but for you to help him, your soon-to-be husband, you have to be able to work calmly with me. Can you do that?"

"Yes, Dr. Clarke," and she took a deep breath.

"Good. Together, we will get through this. When are you going to be married?" he questioned.

"In a week, Dr. Clarke."

"Okay. Can I presume you know all about his health history?"

"Yes, so please don't try to keep anything from me because Dru has never kept any secrets from me, either."

"Then

I can assume you know who his primary care doctor is?"

"Yes, his name is Dr. Benjamin Avery, and his practice is in Chicago, Illinois. I also have his contact information.

"Sharon, you are going to be a wonderful compliment to your husband," and a sense of calm seemed to come over Sharon.

"I have one more question. "Was Dr. Avery the attending physician at Andrew's birth?"

"Yes, Dr. Clarke, he was.

"Oh, thank God," he said, touching Sharon's hand.

"Please call him. I assure you that if you call him, Dr. Avery will come." Dr. Clarke was relieved to hear this.

"Dr. Clarke, could we please see him now? I

promise that we will not disturb him. I need him to know that I am here."

He did agree to it, but only for a few minutes. "He is being prepped for surgery, but no surgery until Dr. Avery arrives. I need him here as soon as possible."

When Sharon stood to walk, the nurse tried to get her to let her push her in the wheelchair, but Sharon wasn't having it. She didn't want Andrew to even sense that he might have to be worried about her in any way.

Lou held Sharon's hand, and they stood at Dru's bedside. "Dru honey, I'm here."

"Ms. Grayson, he has been heavily sedated, and he won't be able to hear you," the nurse said tersely. Maybe not, but she prayed that he would. She wanted to kiss him so badly, but she didn't want to do anything to upset them or be in the way. All she could do was pray that he knew she was there and remember how much she needed him. The nurse must have sensed how helpless she felt and backed away briefly giving her a few more minutes.

"Dru, I'm here. Remember the day you saved my life? You told me that the only thing that mattered to you was that you could not lose me. Remember, honey? Then please come back to me Dru because I cannot live without you."

"Ms. Grayson?" The nurse touched her gently on her shoulder. "You have to leave now, but please know that we will be doing everything humanly possible for your husband," and she escorted them back to the waiting room.

To wait.

About an hour later, she received a text from Dr. Avery saying he was on his way. Louise sat quietly beside her holding her hand. Sharon looked up at her and smiled. There were no words to express what having Lou there meant to Sharon.

"Louise, you've been like a guardian angel sent out to watch over Andrew and I," Sharon told her softly. "Your presence out there in the parking lot today is what saved Dru's life. If you had not been there today watching and acting as quickly as you did, I don't want to think what else Geraldine Peterson may have planned." Louise couldn't stop the tears that burned in her eyes. All she could do was hold on to Sharon's hand and pray.

When Sharon felt her phone vibrate in her pocket, she jumped, it was Nanna. She answered at once. "Sharon, oh my goodness! What is happening out there on your job? It's all over the news." Sharon could hardly speak. Her throat felt like it had been blocked off.

"Nanna, it's Andrew."

"What's happened to Andrew?"

There was no easy way to tell her except to just say it. "His mother shot him, Nanna, and then she killed herself. Dru is critical."

"Oh my God, Sharon! I'm on my way."

Sharon had no idea how she could explain an act so vile. How could any mother try to kill her own son and then take her own life? It was beyond her comprehension. The *why* behind all of this was Andrew's secret. A secret he had lived with all of his life. Now it was left up to her to protect it.

When she looked up and saw Dr. Robinson standing there, she tried to be strong. He touched Lou's hand acknowledging how much her being there meant to him, and she smiled. He held out his hand to Sharon. "Come, Sharon." She was very weak, and he sensed it. They moved to another part of the waiting room that was more private. It bothered him to see Sharon in so much distress.

"This day should be non-existent, Sharon. The Company failed to protect Andrew in so many ways," he said. "All the signs were there, but we failed to keep watch.

Now Andrew, and you too, are the ones paying the price."

Sharon turned and looked at him. She could see the anguish and the sadness in his eyes. "Dr. Robinson, if I can speak for Dru as well as myself, he would tell you that you did not fail us. We love The Company, and that's why we've stayed all of these years. The Company is our family, and when one of us is hurting, we all hurt. We all misjudged what Geraldine was really capable of, and sometimes we fail to see evil in its true form."

Dr. Robinson lowered his head. "Sharon, you are one special woman, always remember that. We are blessed to have you in our lives. Dr. Avery is here, and he asked me to tell you that Dru's surgery has begun." He continued to hold her hand in his. "Sharon, I know in my heart that we will not lose Andrew. He has too much to live for."

She gripped his hand tightly, and when she opened her eyes, she saw Nanna hastily coming toward them. The worry and confusion on her face pained Sharon.

"I'm glad to see you, Naomi," Dr. Robinson said. "You're just what Sharon needs right now," and he cupped her hands in his. He told Sharon he would be back later that day, and to please let him know as soon as Andrew was in recovery. Sharon thanked him for coming, and she would see him soon.

Nanna put her arm around Sharon, and they walked back over to join Louise. "Come and sit down between Lou and I," Nanna said. Shoulders touching between the two of them felt comforting. It was hard for her to even fathom an innocent baby like Andrew entering the world and never experiencing the nurturing of his mother vowing to protect him, even at the risk of her own life. Baby Andrew, never feeling her breath on his face, when she kissed him, or at the moment he left her body and took his first breath, or the gaze of her eyes as she took in every inch of him. Sharon didn't want to talk, move or even breathe. It hurt her so badly. Without doubt, Nanna sensed that. "Let's just sit here, sweetie. Just sit, be quiet, and be still." When they saw Dr. Clarke and Dr. Avery walking towards them, she braced for the worst and prayed for the best.

"The surgery is over. Come, where we can talk." She excused herself from the comfort of Nanna and Louise, and a sharp chill tickled Sharon at the base of her neck and ran down her back, causing her whole body to tremble.

"We will be right here when you return," Nanna told her and took Lou's hand.

Dr. Clarke and Dr. Avery escorted her to a table away from others, one of them on each side of her, and Dr. Avery talked first. "Sharon, Andrew was shot in his lower abdomen. He had an ovary on that side of his body that was completely destroyed and had to be surgically removed. The bullet exited out through his lower back. We believe his mother was trying to destroy any chance of Andrew living a normal life as a man, but ironically, because Andrew has not been under the scrutiny of the medical professionals all of his life, this allowed Andrew's body to pretty much do its own thing. That turned out to be a blessing in disguise. The part she was hoping to destroy is still intact. Nature always has a way of taking care of itself without man's interference.

Andrew has a long recovery ahead of him, and he will need your love and patience. Don't let him try to push you away because he will. You will have to fight this battle with him, and there will be times you will be fighting alone. Just stand strong," and he gripped the back of her hand.

Dr. Clarke spoke next. "Dr. Avery told me that neither of you want children, and that's fine. A lot of time needs to be spent on each other, but just know that there is always that possibility, so birth control is the key. People such as Andrew are a rarity in their own right, and only time will tell what Andrew's body is capable of. Take care of yourself so the two of you can take care of each other. You can see him now but know it will be a while before he regains consciousness because he has been heavily sedated. The first thing he needs to see when he opens his eyes is you."

Dr. Clarke and Dr. Avery accompanied Sharon back to where Lou and Nanna were waiting, and they all went into Andrew's room together. Sharon asked Lou to please call Dr. Robinson and let him know that Andrew was in recovery, and she did. Andrew had been transported to his room and was being closely monitored by a surgical nurse. Dr. Clarke asked her to give them a few minutes and assured her that they would remain there the whole time. The nurse left the room briefly.

The three of them walked over to Dru's bedside, and Sharon touched his hand. "Andrew, I'm here, honey." Dru had survived the surgery, she thought to herself, but did he have the will to live? The heart could only endure so much heartbreak, and that would be their greatest challenge.

Sharon reflected back to the day she so desperately wanted to make things right for Anne, no matter what was wrong with her. As long as they were together, they could fix it.

"No one can ever fix what's wrong with me," Anne told her that day. "No one. Over the years, I had to learn to accept the things I could not change. I am beyond repair." Sharon would never forget the sorrow and defeat in Anne's voice that day, and so much more had hurt him since then.

All that day, Sharon sat at Dru's bedside waiting for some sign of Dru awakening. She remembered that Dr. Clarke said it would take a while for him to start to regain consciousness, but this waiting was driving her crazy. Earlier, Sharon asked Lou and Nanna to go home and rest, and she assured them she would be fine, but she really wasn't fine at all. Tears began to blind her vision, and they annoyed her. She wanted to stay strong for Andrew. He was going to need her to be, so she wiped hard across her eyes in defiance. All she wanted to see was life in her lover's eyes, and that would be enough for now. She got close to his ear and whispered softly, "Dru, I'm here, honey. Please open your eyes." She took his hand in hers and gently squeezed it to stimulate him with her touch. "Please wake up, Dru."

She lay her head down on the bed beside him. If only she could rest, just for a moment, then she would be okay, but in that brief moment, sleep overtook her. A slight nudge against the top of her head aroused her, waking her up with a start. His eyes were open, but it was like he looked right through her. "Dru honey, I'm here. It's Sharon, Andrew. Please wake up all the way, honey." She pushed the button to get the nurse, but Dr. Clarke came immediately.

"He's awake, Dr. Clarke, but not completely." He examined the pupils in his eyes and asked him if he was in any pain.

Andrew closed his eyes again and said nothing. The nurse took his vitals, and everything was stable. Sharon was relieved. Dr. Clarke asked Sharon if she would briefly step out of the room so they could check his wounds and his dressings to make sure there were no problems. She did not want to leave him for a moment, but she also didn't want to be a problem either and risk them asking her to leave for a while because she was not going anywhere.

"You can come right back and stay as long as you wish," Dr. Clarke assured her and asked the nurse if she would arrange for a cot to be brought in so she could stay as long as she liked. "Dr. Clarke, thank you *so* much," she told him. "This will make things easier for me to stay close to Dru because I'm not going anywhere," and he smiled.

Nanna came back that evening and brought her food, clothing, and personal items. They knew what she needed, and she couldn't thank them enough. "Sharon, you know you don't have to thank us for anything," Nanna said. "Nothing will ever keep us away."

Lou went over and touched Dru's hand. "Dru, this is Louise. Please open your eyes." There was no response.

"Sometimes it's hard for me to tell if he's sleeping or just not wanting to interact with me," Sharon said, but then quickly acknowledged that it was probably the pain medication that they were giving him.

Nanna quickly saw how this was affecting Sharon

and took her hand and touched Andrew's. "Dru, it's Nanna, I'm here too. Please come back to us. We all need for you to come back to us. We need you to come back so much, Dru." A single tear formed in the corner of his eye, and he briefly opened his eyes to blink it away then closed them again. "Let him rest, Sharon," Nanna said as she wiped the tears from Sharon's eyes. "He knows we are here for him honey," and she led Sharon away. All they could do was sit there and draw strength from each other.

Finally, Nanna hated to, but she told Sharon she would probably have to be leaving soon before dark set in. "I don't like being out after dark," and Sharon fully understood. "I'll be back tomorrow, though," she reassured her. "The next day, and the next, until Andrew comes home." Nanna hugged Sharon and told her she loved her and to stay strong. She went over and kissed Dru on the cheek. "I love you, Andrew. Please come back to all of us soon."

Louise walked out with Nanna and told her she would be staying with Sharon for a while longer trying to keep her mind off of things, and Nanna was grateful. "Sharon really needs that right now, Lou, but more than anything else, thank you Louise for being such a good friend to both of them. Your caring for them is unconditional, and that's what true friendship is all about." Nanna hugged Lou. "Qualities like yours Louise are a true treasure. Never lose them."

After Nanna left, Lou's heart felt full. The nurse came in and wanted to get Andrew settled and give him his bedtime meds, so they went out into one of the family waiting rooms to talk. It was time for Sharon to know as much as she could about Anne Marie Peterson's life, and if anyone could tell her, it would be Lou.

16

Louise sat there for what seemed like hours as if she were reliving the past. "We grew up in the slums of Chicago. It wasn't the best of times for any of us, but for Anne Marie, she never had a chance." Lou propped her bare feet up in the seat and wrapped her arms around her knees.

"When I was a kid, I remember listening to some of the old women talk about a woman named Geraldine who was a prostitute, and the pimp that turned her out was from Africa. They used to say that he had bad blood, and that was the reason Anne Marie was born the way she was. It was creepy listening to some of the stuff they were saying, especially when you're a child, but those old folks' tails were riddled with a lot of half-truths and untruths. Anne briefly went to the same primary school I went to but in a lower grade because she was behind. She really did act weird though and stayed to herself a lot. She seemed so lost at times and so overwhelmed, like she didn't know what to do or how to act, just lost. Sometimes poverty and being considered an oddity doesn't mix well, leaving you separated from the rest of society, and that was Anne Marie. She was an attractive child even then, tall, long legged, but always stayed slouched against something or sitting or partially camouflaged, never taking a proud stance."

Lou paused for a moment like she was reliving it all over again. After a long silence, she said, "I can't imagine how completely debilitating that had to be for a child Anne's age having to be forced to hide a secret so disgusting. That would be enough to make anyone act weird."

Lou rested her head on her forearms as if she were trying to force the very thought out of her brain. "I'll bet Anne wasn't at that school no more than three or four months at the most, and when they went out on Christmas break, she never came back. They disappeared from the neighborhood, and she never saw Anne Marie again, which didn't surprise her because people started talking about why she missed so much school. That's when Child Protective Services started nosing around, calling Anne into the office and asking her questions. When people began getting suspicious or getting too close, they would just disappear. How sad life must have been for Anne, Sharon. I remember trying to talk to her at recess time, but Anne seemed fearful and intimidated by me and because she was incredibly unkept, that's probably a lot of the reasons she stayed so obscure."

"During those years, my parents didn't have a lot either," Lou said, "But the one thing we had that Anne Marie didn't, was parents who loved us unconditionally and showed us that every day. They raised us with a positive mind set and lots of love. That's the most valuable commodity you could ever send a child out into the world with, is love."

Sharon's heart felt like it would burst with sorrow for what Anne had endured, and so did Louise, and it was so obvious now what a profound effect it had on Louise. "No child should ever have to live with that kind of suffering," Lou said. "It's like being locked in a caged mind with no way of escape, really, for the last forty-five years."

"That would be enough to create demons in anyone's head, and I understand now that this job at The Company is what saved Andrew's life," Sharon said.

"To a certain extent, that's true, Sharon. The Company became a refuge, escape, and hiding place, but he never really healed from the trauma. Anne Marie Peterson never really existed. It was just a label, a form of identity, like a social security number. Andrew was never truly brought to life until you, Sharon. Over the years when you became supervisor over the department Anne worked in, I could see the bond growing between the two of you," Lou remembered. "Pleasing you and not wanting to disappoint you made Anne Marie come alive inside, and that day on the employee outing when you fell and hurt yourself really badly, there was something between the two of you that day that neither of you could hide. It was as if there was no one else in the world but the two of you. Anne loved you so much Sharon, she was willing to risk her own life to save yours, and everyone knew it."

Sharon pressed the heels of her hands against her eye sockets and sobbed. "Lou, if I lose Dru, nothing will ever be the same for me anymore. Anne is what has finally made me feel complete as well."

Lou knew how much this was hurting Sharon. "Andrew's seeming rejection, not making eye contact, telling you to go away, maybe not verbally right now, but emotionally, is tearing you apart, but Sharon, please don't take it personally. If Andrew thinks he is not going to be the man he wants to be for you, he will try to run you away. He will not let you settle for anything less."

That night after Louise left, Sharon decided to call Dr. Avery the next morning and ask him to please come. She felt if she could just convince Dru that his manhood had not been affected at all and share with him everything that he and Dr. Clarke had shared with her, maybe that would make a big difference in the success of his recovery. She prayed so hard that it would.

Sharon was beside herself with grief, she couldn't sleep. After she thought Andrew was asleep, she decided to take a shower, and try to calm herself. She dimmed the lights, undressed and got into the shower. She immediately felt her body uncoil itself as the warm water covered her body, and she felt so much better. After getting out, she stepped into the room to dry off and she didn't know why at first, but a strange feeling came over her. She could feel Andrew's eyes on her body, caressing every inch of her. She pretended not to notice, but through the full-length mirror on the door, she could see Dru's eyes open. Knowing he was watching made her hot all over. She never acknowledged that she knew. She got dressed and laid down on the cot and soon fell asleep.

The next morning when the nurse came in, she used that opportunity to leave and call Dr. Avery. When his receptionist answered, Sharon explained that she really needed to talk to him directly, and she transferred her. She asked him to please forgive her for bothering him so much, but if he could please come and talk to Andrew about the things she felt might be hindering his progress. He assured her that she was not bothering him at all, and in fact, he and Dr. Clarke had the same concerns. He was planning on coming down this weekend to check on him, and it wasn't an inconvenience at all. They were hoping to release him in a couple of weeks or so if he continued to improve. Sharon knew he was trying to lift her spirits and give her something to hold on to, but Dru was so distant from her, and it hurt her deeply.

She thanked Dr. Avery and told him she was really looking forward to seeing him. Dr. Avery instructed Sharon to remain strong and to remember that she was not in this alone. He reiterated that he would see her over the weekend. "Thank you so much, Dr. Avery." When she went back up to Andrew's room, she decided against saying anything to him about Haven House or her conversation with Dr. Avery. If only she could get him to acknowledge her. She knew that it wasn't the medication making him so distant from her. She could only hope that once he was released from the hospital and they got back to Haven House, they would work their way back to each other.

After the nursing staff finished up with everything they needed to do, she went back into Andrew's room and went over to his bedside. His eyes were open, and he did not look past her this time. In fact, he looked directly at her and spoke. "Sharon, please go away." Even if he had slapped her across her face, that still wouldn't have wounded her as much as those three words did. They stung intensely.

"Please go away," he said again, but she didn't budge, and then he closed his eyes and didn't open them again. She sat down in the chair beside his bed and didn't respond for a long time, trying to recover from the shock. His rejection injured her for sure, but she also knew that was his intention. She decided to address Andrew's request. "If this is what you want Andrew, then tell me you never loved me at all. Open your eyes and look at me. Tell me that you took my virginity from me, and you don't want me anymore, and I will leave." Tears streamed down Sharon's face.

He tried to turn his head away, but he couldn't, so he just closed his eyes and refused to open them again. The rest of the day, the both of them were in pain, physically and mentally. She sat there for most of the day until her cell vibrated in her pocket. She stepped out of the room to answer. It was a text from Dr. Avery.

"Dr. Avery, where are you?"

"I'm here in St. Louis."

"Dr. Avery...."

"I'll see you soon," he texted back.

What Sharon had said about having one or two true friends was an understatement. As soon as Dr. Avery and Dr. Clarke showed up that evening, she left the room and went to the hospital chapel looking for peace and strength to keep her strong. Sometimes all one can do is sit back and work through the pain. Sharon sat stoically in the chapel and lost all sense of time. It was peaceful and quiet, completely separated from the rest of the hospital. She didn't want to move, and her brain felt completely drained of any energy. She began to weep softly. When she felt her cell vibrate in her pocket, it startled her, and she got up and walked out of the chapel and answered.

"Sharon, where are you?" It was Dr. Avery. She told him she was in the hospital chapel. "Just stay put, I will come to you," he said.

"Come Sharon, we need to talk," he said softly. They found a quiet place to sit and for a while, he didn't say anything, but finally, he spoke. "Sharon, Dr. Clarke and I had a long talk with Andrew, as well as giving him a thorough examination. That's what took longer than we expected. His wounds are healing well, but what we are really concerned about is his mental health. We assured him that his manhood was intact, and in fact, because we surgically removed the ovary on the left side, will even make a bigger difference, but it will take time for Andrew to see. We told him to let nature take its course in his body like it always had. Dr. Clarke and I will be releasing him in another week. The problem is he does not want to go back to Haven House. Is his place still intact and available?"

"Oh my God, no, Dr. Avery. It is not." Sharon was frantic. They had donated all of Andrew's furniture, and they were in the process of turning in their sixty-day notices to the leasing agencies. Sharon felt like she was losing all control.

Dr. Avery knew she was at her breaking point, and she surrendered to her defeat. He took her hand in his and asked, "Sharon, do you have your car here?"

"Yes, I do. Louise and Nanna brought it to me last week just in case I needed it."

"Good, now this is what I want you to do, " Dr. Avery continued. "I want you to get in your car and leave the hospital for the rest of the day."

"Oh no, Dr. Avery, I can't do that. Andrew needs me."

"Sharon, that's the point. Yes, he does, and he needs to start realizing that he does," and Dr. Avery insisted that she do as he asked. "Sharon, if you don't get a handle on your own mental stability, you won't be able to help Andrew at all. Can't you see that? In fact, after giving it some further thought, I am going to talk to Dr. Clarke again before he leaves, and maybe it would be better for the both of you if we keep Andrew an extra week and start his physical therapy. Andrew needs to start bearing weight, taking steps, finding his balance, and gaining his strength back before we release him. We will start on Monday and continue with it even after he goes home. Now, for you young lady, when we come on Monday morning, I want you to leave the hospital and go back to work. Your employer needs you too, and you can come back in the evenings and continue to build your relationship with Andrew. He needs to start missing you. Come, let me walk you to your car," he said. Dr. Avery was not taking no for an answer.

"Dr. Avery, I can't just up and leave right now."

"Yes, you can, Sharon. You have not left this hospital in over a week." Sharon's heart was flooded with emotions.

"After we have gotten Andrew settled for the

evening, you can come back. Someone has to start taking care of you too, and we have to start by getting you back to work. You just got that new promotion, and you need to start earning it."

"Oh, my goodness, Dr. Avery. Would you believe I had forgotten all about my promotion? Dr. Robinson hasn't said anything to you, has he Dr. Avery?" Sharon was beside herself. "How could I forget something so important, really, to the both of them?"

"Now Sharon, you know that's not the case at all. This is just something I want you to do. It's understandable that you have blocked out everything and everyone but Andrew. You have too much on your plate," he told her in no uncertain terms. "I also know all too well what your positions at The Company mean to the both of you. So, let's put our heads together and make it work, okay?"

"Okay, Dr. Avery."

Dr. Avery continued. "I realize now that helping Andrew build his strength is the most important first step. Right now, he feels like he is not going to be the same man he was before all of this happened, and it scares him to death, but everything is going to be fine, Sharon. Just know I won't let anything happen to Andrew, so please go home, get the things you need for tomorrow, and get yourself ready for next week. Andrew will be coming home with you to Haven House."

Sharon finally accepted that Dr. Avery was not taking no for an answer, but more than anything else, he had given her hope. She hated to leave Andrew, even for a couple of hours, but she knew what Dr. Avery was saying was right. His wisdom and guidance in their lives right now was just what they both needed. They walked slowly to the parking garage, both in deep thought. After they located Sharon's car, he went on. "Sharon, you and Andrew are alike in so many ways; however, you were fortunate enough to have very loving parents but lost them when you needed them most. But Andrew? Unfortunately, he has never known that kind of love until you. Now he would give it all up before he let it destroy what the two of you have. It is his way of trying to survive. Let me help you and Andrew, Sharon. You aren't aware of this, but I have never had the pleasure of having children. Just like you and Andrew, my wife and I were career seekers and continued to put it off. When she passed away, it left me with a tremendous void in my life. The two of you have become the children I never had if you don't mind me saying."

"Oh, Dr. Avery." She hugged him and cried. "You being in our lives is such a natural thing. It's just as simple as that. You have actually become that parental link in our lives, and when we desperately needed you, you were there, just as simple and unforced as that."

"You go home and rest, Sharon. Please understand that I have Andrew's best interests at heart. He deserves the best, and the best is you." Dr. Avery stood there in the parking garage until Sharon could no longer see him. Being with him today enlivened her in so many ways, but more comforting than anything else, they had a guardian angel watching over them, and for that, she was truly grateful.

17

When Sharon arrived at Haven House, an overpowering feeling of emptiness seemed to swallow her up leaving her with a hollow feeling in her stomach. It was almost June, but she felt unusually cold and empty on the inside to her. It reminded her of the way it felt before she ever brought Andrew there. Even though it was completely furnished, she knew she could never live there without Andrew. What once brought her so much joy and comfort, left her not knowing what to do with herself.

She went into the bedroom and laid down on Dru's side of the bed, trying to feel his presence with all her might. She missed him dearly. The last day they were intimate was the day in the shower. Her memories drifted to a time of exhilaration and expectation of a wonderful and full life.

It didn't take long for weariness to overtake her, and

when she woke, she only had enough time to gather clothes for work, which consisted of a couple of sweats and T-shirts to sleep in, and personal items. Sharon had always taken so much pride in her appearance, especially at work, but lately, that was the last thing she cared about. She had to get it together for the rest of the week if she was going back to work. Tomorrow after work, she would have no choice but to come back out to Haven House and pull a week's worth of clothes together.

Dr. Avery had made such a difference in their lives, and she could see the bond between Dr. Avery and Andrew growing since the day they went to see him in Chicago. It was akin to being reunited with a lost child, and there was something about Dr. Avery that Sharon liked from their very first meeting. He not only had Andrew's best interests at heart, but hers as well.

When she got back to the hospital, Andrew was sitting up in a chair that supported his back while they changed his bedding. She wished she had waited a little longer because he seemed uncomfortable. She went over and sat down beside him, kissed him and whispered against his mouth, "I love you, Dru." He didn't look past her this time, and he didn't turn away. She could tell he had been wondering where she was. When the nurses were ready to lay him back down, she left the room. Once the nurses came out and told her they had given him something to help him relax, Sharon was glad. Things had been uncomfortably strained between them lately, she didn't or wasn't sure how to behave around him anymore. She asked the nurse how he was doing otherwise, and all she would say was better.

When Sharon went back into the room, she dimmed the lights and sat down in the same chair he had been sitting in, just close enough for him to be able to see her. She downloaded mellow mood music on her phone and played it softly so he could hear it. When Barry White's "Can't Get Enough of Your Love, Baby" came on, he opened his eyes and looked at her like he had not seen her for a very long time, then sleep overtook him. When he woke the next morning, she was already dressed for work. She went over and kissed him longer this time. "I'm so in love with you, Dru," and he returned her kiss. He never took his eyes from her the whole time. The sparkle from the ring on her finger caught his attention, and he wondered how long it had been. He'd lost all perception of time.

"I'm going to work today, honey," she said softly, "But as soon as I pick up clothes from Haven House for work tomorrow, I will be back here, and then we'll talk, okay?" She hated to leave him, but it was important that she did. She had work to do, but so did he. She left, without saying another word.

The first thing she did when she got to The Company was stop by Dr, Robinson's office before she went to hers. When she walked in, the receptionist greeted her warmly. "Is Dr. Robinson here yet, Marie?"

"He sure is Sharon, and he will be very happy to see you," she responded back.

"Thanks, Marie."

She knocked lightly on the door, and when he

opened it and saw her, he was, "very happy to see her. "Sharon, it is so good to see you. Come, sit down. How are things going with Andrew?"

"Slowly, Dr. Robinson, and he is not handling things very well right now."

"I'm aware. I stopped by yesterday," he said, "But Dr. Clarke and Dr. Avery were there. I told Andrew I would be back today, and I will."

"Thank you, Dr. Robinson, for everything." She acknowledged that she had been gone from work much longer than she intended to be and told him that Dr. Avery graciously reminded her that she had her new position waiting on her, and she needed to start earning it.

Dr. Robinson laughed in his easy-going way and said, "That sounds like Benjamin. Sharon, you look wonderful, and you definitely fit the position well." She thanked him. She needed that confidence booster so much right now, and he touched her hand. "Anytime, Sharon. Things may seem overwhelming right now, but it will get better. In the meantime, I am so happy to have you back, and if I don't see you anymore today, I will get together with you tomorrow. I really want to get out of here a little earlier today and spend some time with Andrew." That made Sharon happy.

Being back at work after all that happened seemed strained. She left her car parked up front in the main parking lot. She didn't know if she would ever be able to park again where everything happened. The walk from the main building did her good. She texted Lou and told her she was back to work and that made Lou so happy. Sharon could tell when people's caring was genuine, and Lou's was.

"Let's do lunch today," Lou texted back. "My treat."

"Come on up when you're ready, and thanks, Lou."

When she walked into the reception area, Chrystal was caught a bit off guard. Sharon wasn't ready to deal with prying eyes and questions not asked, but she knew she'd better get ready for it. "Hi Sharon, I'm so happy to have you back," she said. "Damn, Sharon, you've really lost weight. How is Anne doing?"

"Coming along. She still has a lot of ground to cover, but she's strong."

"I heard about your new promotion, girl," she said. "It's good to know that with a little hard work, The Company sure has your back." Sharon picked up on the sarcastic overtones, but she just let it run off like water running off of a duck's back.

"Thanks, Chrystal. Well, like Anne would say, I'd better start earning my keep around here," and they both smiled. "Let me know if you need anything, Chrystal. I'm sorry I have been gone for so long, so if there's anything, just ask." Then she quickly escaped to her office until lunch time.

Louise texted Sharon to let her know she was on her way. "See you in a few." Sharon texted her back and asked her if she wouldn't mind picking her up in the main parking lot because that's where she had parked her car.

"No problem, Sis. See you in a few."

Sharon gathered herself together and went up front to Chrystal's desk. "I'll see you in a bit Chrystal. I have business up front, but I'll be back soon if you need anything."

Right now, she felt like a fish out of water floundering about, not really on point like she usually was. It was distracting, but today was only her first day back, and just like Dr. Robinson said earlier, it would get better. She sure as hell hoped so.

Those little walks between buildings were wonderful. They seemed to clear her head and bring her body back to life. Right now, she needed that because she felt like there was a battle of wills going on inside her that she was coming close to losing.

She got up front and saw Lou waiting. "Hey friend," she said.

"Hey, back atcha," Sharon replied back, and they both laughed.

"Sharon, you are as thin as a rail. We're going to have to put some meat on them bones before Andrew gets out."

"So, I've been told. Chrystal said the same thing earlier. I haven't had any appetite lately. You know, Dru did all the cooking," she reminded Lou. "I absolutely loved it."

"Well, he's going to have to hurry up and get better before you starve to death, and the first person he'll try to blame is me," and they both laughed. It felt so good. Being with Lou was easy, and that's what she needed right now, easy.

"Lou, what's your take on Chrystal?" Sharon asked out of the blue. "She's always been nice to me, Sharon continued, "But there's something I can't quite put my finger on. Remember the day she walked in on a conversation between the two of them talking about Anne that day?"

"Yes, I remember, but I really can't say, though," Lou replied back.

Sharon knew that Lou was not the type to bad mouth someone unjustly, and that was one of the things Sharon liked about Lou. "I don't want to alienate her in any way. You know that old saying, Lou, 'you can kill a person with kindness?"

"Now ain't that the truth," Lou said. "Well, I do know that Chrystal has been at The Company for five years as a regular staff member. Then she took the receptionist position down in your building, remember?" Lou asked.

"Yes, I seem to recollect that now that you mention it. I had forgotten all about that until you reminded me. She has been asking about Anne in a roundabout way," Sharon said, "But of course, so have a lot of people."

"That's the truth," Lou said and continued on, "They don't want the gossip to get out of hand if they don't want Dr. Robinson on their asses. He hates that shit, and I'm glad.

I hate gossip. Chrystal knows you care a lot about Anne, Sharon, and you always have, so that's nothing out of the norm."

"Yea Lou, but with everything that happened with Anne's mother and the things she said that day, how are we expected to keep something like that under wraps, Louise?" Sharon seemed distraught, and Lou tried to relieve some of her anxieties. "If you want an honest opinion, Sharon, slim and none."

"I know Lou, you're right."

"I know why you parked up here in the main parking lot instead of down in our own parking area, Sharon and believe me, I understand. It's going to take a while before you feel comfortable with parking back down there. Just give it some time," Lou suggested.

"Has anyone down in your building asked you about that day, Lou?" Sharon asked.

"Sharon, people pretty much know me well enough not to come to me with that shit." That made Sharon laugh.

"I know that's the truth!" Sharon responded back and laughed.

"Lou, can I ask you something, and all you have to say is yes or no?"

"What is with you today, Sharon, twenty questions?" and then she laughed.

"I promise this is the last thing, but it's something I

have to know before I put my foot in my mouth."

"What is it Sharon?" she asked.

"Lou, when my new promotion really takes off, I'm going to need someone in my old position I can fully trust. If I recommend you to Dr. Robinson for the supervisory position, would you be willing to accept it?" I really hope you will."

Louise almost ran up on the curb when she turned the corner. She pulled the car over and parked.

"Sharon, are you serious?"

"Of course, I'm serious. I would love it if you would be willing to come down and work with me, Andrew and Chrystal. I know it will be a while before Dru will be able to return to work, but if Chrystal is as good a team player as I hope she is, we could have the best running department on campus. Dr. Robinson told me that I can select whomever I think is qualified for the position, and Lou, you are more than qualified. Please say you'll do it."

Louise was in a state of shock. "Sharon, I had no idea how much this meant to you. I guess I didn't realize how much respect you have for me, not only as a friend, but as another woman who you feel is deserving of this opportunity." After Lou got over her shock, she said. "You know, Sharon, it really doesn't surprise me that you would do something like this because it's truly who you are as a person."

"Lou, you deserve this. Nanna always taught me that

we should share the love, and Lou, Andrew and I love you very much. Thank you for being our friend," and she touched Lou's hand.

Sharon told Louise that before she left today, she would let Dr. Robinson know who she had selected to be her new supervisor, and as soon as she got everything worked out, she would call her before the end of the day.

After Sharon got back to her office, she wanted to leave early more than anything, but resisted the temptation. She wanted to get everything finalized for Louise and the sooner the better. She knew it wouldn't be a problem, and once she got it settled, that would be one less thing on her plate that needed to be resolved.

The rest of the day went fast. She wanted to call and check on Dru, but she decided against it. Things had been so strained between them lately, so about 4:00 p.m., she decided to call Dr. Robinson to see if he was available to talk with her, plus she had other things to take care of in the business office. If everything went the way she hoped for, then she would be able to leave for the day.

"Yes, Sharon, I'm free. Come on up," he said.

She thanked him and told him she was on her way. Getting Lou hired in her position would be the icing on the cake on her first day back.

"Hi Sharon," Marie greeted her, "Go on back, he's expecting you." She knocked lightly on his door. "Come on in, Sharon."

She told him she would not hold him very long, but she wanted to let him know who she thought would be the perfect fit for her position that would be opening up soon. "She has been with The Company for ten years, and has given them nothing but loyal service, plus, she is a wonderful person."

"Sharon, I'm so glad you brought this up, because there is someone I've been thinking about as well," he said. I know I told you the final decision would be yours to make, and that still stands. It's your department that will have to work with that person, but I want to run it by you. The final decision is still yours to make."

Sharon's breath caught in her throat, but she managed to say that whoever he had in mind would be a good candidate as well.

"I hope you will be happy with my recommendation. I feel strongly that Louise Russell has also given this company exemplary service, and I believe it is time for her to get the chance to put her talents to work."

Sharon could hardly contain her excitement. All she could remember hearing was Louise Russell's name. Before she knew it, she was on her feet and went over and gave Dr. Robinson the biggest hug. "Oh, Dr. Robinson, that's exactly who she was talking about as well. I couldn't be any happier to hear you feel the same way."

Dr. Robinson laughed so hard. "Well, Sharon, I presumed we were on the same page."

"Yes, we are, but haven't we always been Dr.?

Sharon replied with a huge smile on her face.

"Yes, Sharon, we are, and oh, by the way, it's good to have you back." Sharon thanked him and as she was on her way out of his office, turned and told Dr. Robinson that she would see him tomorrow.

Sharon was happier than she had been since the day of her promotion and wedding proposal. She felt like she would burst if she didn't tell Lou the good news right away. She called Lou's cell vocalizing, "Please answer, Lou."

"Hey Sharon, what's up?"

"Lou, you got the position!"

"What? Are you sure?"

"Hold on Sharon, my phone is ringing. I'll call you back."

"Okay Lou, but don't forget."

It seemed like it took Lou forever to get back with her. About fifteen minutes later her cell rang, and it was Lou. She could tell she had been crying. "Lou, is everything okay?"

"Sharon, everything is better than okay. That was Dr. Robinson on the phone, and you are now talking to your new supervisor. He told me that both of you agreed that I am perfect for the position, and I accepted. Sharon, you have changed my life today," Lou told her between tears. "I don't know how to thank you and Dr. Robinson, but know, I will never give you any cause to be disappointed in your decision. I promise," and both of them were crying.

18

Sharon could hardly wait to get to the hospital and share the good news with Dru. She didn't even want to think about going all the way to Haven House only to get clothes for the rest of the week. It would take too long and would be almost dark by the time she got back to the hospital. She decided to stop at the mall. It was no distance to the hospital from there, and it would be worth the few extra dollars on two or three outfits to tide her over through the rest of the week. Since she had just received the promotion to Executive Administrator over Marketing, she had no choice but to look the part.

She made a quick turn into the mall parking lot. It shouldn't take her long at all to pick up a few things. She already knew what she was looking for. Where she shopped, one of the associates would be more than happy to assist her. She wanted to get to the hospital as soon as possible. In as little as an hour, she had everything she needed and more. She chose the outfit she wanted for the next day, and the rest she locked in the trunk of her car. When she pulled into the hospital parking garage, it wasn't even 6:00 p.m. yet. Had she gone to Haven House first, she would just be leaving at this time if she had gone home.

When she got up to Andrew's room, they had him sitting up in a chair again, and she thought that may be part of his therapy. This time, they kept him up longer but checked on him more frequently. She pulled her chair close up in front of him, and he didn't seem to be in as much pain as he was yesterday. She kissed him and told him she was going to change into something comfortable, and she would be right back. She had sweats and T-shirts in the closet that would be ideal, and she wasted no time getting back to him.

Things seemed much more relaxed between them today, and she was hopeful that was a good sign. She missed the way Dru used to touch her and wondered if it would ever be that way between them again. His mother had taken so much from them.

"Honey, guess what? Louise got her supervisory position," she said with so much excitement she could hardly contain herself. When Andrew smiled and touched her hand, that simple gesture from him caused her to take hold of his hand and not let go. "I recommended her to Dr. Robinson," she continued, "And he agreed that she would be the perfect candidate. Lou was so excited, Dru, and grateful. It made me feel so good to see her so excited. Now we can hold down the fort until you come back," she told him. "We are going to be one heck of a team, Dru. Even Dr. Robinson was saying today that you would be on the mend and back in no time at all, and he can hardly wait." When Andrew smiled, she came alive inside. "She'd missed that sexy smile so much."

"He came by this evening," Andrew said. "He just left before you got here."

Sharon beamed with happiness. "I knew he was coming," she said casually. "He told me he was."

"I was happy to see him," he said.

After a while, he seemed aloof and quiet. She knew he had started therapy today and wondered if he could be having some pain and just wasn't saying. When the nurse came in and asked him if he was ready to lay down, he shook his head no, which was a surprise to the nurses.

"Mr. Grayson, are you sure?" and they paused for a moment. "Well, we'll come back in a bit," they said.

"Dru honey, you started therapy today. Aren't you tired?" He didn't say anything. He used the remote that moved his chair in the sitting position then he held out both of his hands to Sharon. Sharon stood directly in front of him and took both of his hands in hers. She was so scared. If

Andrew got hurt, she would never forgive herself.

"Honey, please be careful." Let me call the nurse," but he said, "No, not yet." Sharon gripped his hands tightly and pulled until he was in a standing position. "Dru, please be careful." He took her in his arms. "Sharon, you are so thin." It didn't surprise her that he would notice, and she immediately tried to explain.

He brushed her hair back away from her face like he used to and looked deeply into her eyes. "Please take care of yourself until I can, please." She seriously needed this, and feeling his arms around her, her whole body came back to life. Tears blinded them. They could feel the love flowing through their bodies when they kissed. They were holding on to each other when the nurses came back into the room. They thought they were going to have a heart attack. They rushed over and helped Dru walk the short distance to the bed and as soon as they got him settled, they gave him something to help him relax.

Of course, Sharon already knew she was on the hot seat. "Ms. Grayson, please be careful. We don't want you to get hurt, and we sure don't want Mr. Grayson to get hurt either. He is making so much progress, as you can see, but he still has a long way to go," she said.

"I'm sorry," Sharon said. I promise I will not let him talk me into anything like this again. I just think he wanted to hold me in his arms, if only for a little while. I have to admit, it felt so good." The nurses looked at the two of them and smiled.

"Good night you two," they said and left the room.

The next morning when she went over and kissed him lightly on the lips, he awoke. She told him she was leaving for work, but as soon as work was over, she would be back. Andrew told her that he missed her so much when she was gone, and it broke her heart. "When will you be back?" he asked.

"Soon, honey," she promised. "You work hard in rehab today, Dru. "I know it's hard, but it will only make you stronger every day. I will be back before you know it." With that, she turned and left the room. It pained her to see him this way, but they both had a battle to win, and this battle they would be fighting together.

When Sharon got to work, she parked in her own parking lot in defiance. It was time for her to face her own demons. No longer was Dru's mother going to continue to control their lives, even in death, and that's exactly what they were letting her do.

When she walked into the reception area, Chrystal was already at her desk. Sharon greeted her with a smile. "Hi Sharon, Anne must be doing better," she said. "I can tell by that big smile you have on your face."

"Yes, so much better," Sharon told her. "She still has a long way to go, but there is great progress in her recovery."

"Sharon, that dress is fantastic," Chrystal took notice. "Simple, but chic. You have excellent taste." Sharon thanked her.

With the new promotion, they all were going to have a lot to learn. It would still be a while before Anne came back, but she would be back. They would have to keep things running smoothly until she did. She could even work from home if Dr. Robinson okayed it, and that would be a big help. Chrystal agreed, and she knew Dr. Robinson would say yes. Sharon knew that this would be the right time to tell Chrystal that she and Dr. Robinson had selected the new supervisor to take over her position. "Chrystal, I hope you agree that Louise Russell will be a wonderful asset to our department and someone great to work with. I believe that since you seem to like Louise, you will be comfortable with her becoming a part of our team. Her years of service and her work ethic makes her the perfect candidate," Sharon concluded. Chrystal said nothing.

"Chrystal, I was just telling Dr. Robinson yesterday that I couldn't have asked for a better team to work with, and you do realize that being the receptionist will not be your only responsibility," Sharon went on. "This is going to be the perfect opportunity for you to learn a lot about The Company as well as our department. So, by all means, get ready Chrystal because we are all going to be learning together."

Chrystal finally spoke. "Sharon, thank you so much. You have a way about you that makes people feel worthwhile, but can I speak frankly?" she asked.

"Yes, of course, Chrystal, I wouldn't want it any other way."

"Sharon, "I know that you really don't feel as

comfortable with me as you do with Louise and Anne, and that's fine, but I know with all of us working together, we are going to make this department a force to be reckoned with," Chrystal stated, and just that gesture made Sharon feel so much better and remove that invisible block between them

Sharon said, "Chrystal, please forgive me if she'd seem standoffish at times. There has been so much going on lately, and if she came off that way she didn't mean to be, but I want you to know that. That's not the way I am at all."

Chrystal quickly agreed. "I know you're not Sharon, and I do understand. When someone you care about is hurting, like Anne for instance, it hurts you as well. I do know how much you care about Anne."

"That's true Chrystal, but let's make something clear. We are a family, and I would feel it as strongly if it were Louise or you or Dr. Robinson, okay?"

Sharon knew it was time for her to excuse herself because she didn't feel comfortable with the way this was going. She could sense the undertones. "Chrystal, we will get together and have a meeting soon and start planning new strategies for production within the department. It will probably be a week or so before Louise can officially move up here," she continued. "She wants to help her department find the right person for her spot, but we will be fine. Anne should be released soon, but she will still have a physical therapist coming in everyday to do strength building and to work on mobility. She has her work cut out for her, but she is a fighter."

"Tell Anne I asked about her," Chrystal said. "I will give Louise a call and congratulate her as well. We'll talk soon, Sharon, and thanks."

Sharon wasn't quite sure how to take Chrystal, and Chrystal probably felt the same way about her. Only time would tell. She could only hope that spending time with Chrystal today and reminding her that she, too, would be playing an integral role in the success of their department would create a feeling of her being a valued team member. Everyone needs to feel valued, and that's what she wanted for all of her team members.

About 4:00 p.m., Sharon decided to leave early. She wanted to get to the hospital earlier today, and she felt pulled in a million different directions. This morning when she left, Andrew seemed lost and scared, but so did she. She would be glad when they could go home to Haven House together. It seemed so long since they were there, and she missed it so much. The morning of the shooting flashed through her mind and an intense fear engulfed her. She immediately pushed it away and focused on the present. She couldn't bear to think about that day. Before she left work, she took out what she would wear the next day as well as something appropriate for the hospital. She wanted to spend as much time with Dru as she could. That was all that mattered now.

When she got off of the elevator, the nurse told her Andrew had a very good day and that made Sharon feel so much better. When she opened the door, he was in bed, but he was wide awake. "Hi honey, what did you do, sneak away early?" he joked and laughed.

"I'll never tell," she joked back and smiled with a guilty look on her face. "Well, your timing is perfect. Guess who just left?" Sharon answered, "Dr. Robinson?"

"You guessed it. It was so good to see him again. He is sure smitten with you. I don't have anything to worry about, do I honey?" and he had the nerve to laugh.

"Boy, you are definitely feeling your oats today." She chuckled. "Andrew, what have you been drinking today?" and when she said that they both fell over laughing with gusto.

One of the nurses stuck her head in the door and smiled. "Is everything okay in there?" she asked. "I'm sorry," Sharon apologized. "My husband seems to be getting back to his old self," she giggled. Sharon laughed so hard, she almost lost her breath, and Dru just laid there with an innocent look on his face. He quickly changed the subject.

"Honey, you'll never guess what else Dr. Robinson said. He said that when I'm released from the hospital, besides my physical therapist three days a week, he is having a massage therapist come out to Haven House to give me deep muscle massages to keep my muscles relaxed. That will keep me from having problems with muscle spasms. They will be coming in between my physical therapy days."

Sharon was super excited. "Honey, that is so awesome," she told him. Seeing Andrew this way was everything she could have ever hoped for. "It will help me get back on my feet so much faster," he said excitedly. Sharon, are you aware that Dr. Robinson blames himself for what happened? Did you know that?"

"Yes, honey, I did."

It angered Andrew that Dr. Robinson felt like he was to blame. "I told Dr. Robinson to please not let my mother continue to hurt any of us anymore than she already has, and that I will be back to work before he knew it. As long as I have you, I can do anything," he said quietly. Andrew was bursting with excitement knowing he was being released from the hospital on Friday. Dr. Clarke and Dr. Avery told him the good news when they came to see him.

19

Sharon noticed she had missed a text message from Dr. Robinson. His message read as follows, "I am aware that Andrew is being released from the hospital on Friday, and I believe it is best for you to be with him. This is a very special day for both of you. Monday will be our big day. I would like to get with you, Chrystal Johnson, and Louise Russell tomorrow around 10:00 a.m. After that, I recommend you spend some quality time with Andrew.

He continued, "If it's the last thing I ever do, Sharon, I want to see Andrew become the real person he was meant to be. Nature can be cruel sometimes, but it never makes mistakes, only we do. I care about the two of you immensely, and what you have brought to The Company came from your deep desire to help others. Andrew has lived a life of nothing but pain, humiliation, and abuse. You gave him the one thing he knew nothing about and that was unconditional love. I'll meet you in your office at 10:00 a.m. tomorrow. Let the rest of the ladies know. Rest well."

Sharon was moved to tears by Dr. Robinson's message. She could not have asked for a more loving and compassionate person to work with than he. About eighty percent of the people who work for The Company are long-term employees, ten years or more, and that's probably why.

Sharon had so much on her mind. If she could lay close to Dru and feel his body close to hers, that would make all the difference. In two more days, they would be back home at Haven House. Before she tried to get to sleep, she sent texts to Louise and Chrystal. "See you tomorrow at 10 a.m. Dr. Robinson wants to have a short meeting with the three of us. Lunch after, my treat."

It didn't take long for Louise to text back. "Gotcha, boss lady." Louise was so funny, and her message brought a smile to Sharon's face. A few minutes later, Chrystal's came through. "I'm already there, remember? I'm the new trainee. No call-ins allowed for me." Sharon just loved them.

At some point, Sharon must have dropped off to sleep, but she sure didn't feel rested. She felt as if she had been drugged. It was quiet at the nurse's station because they had not changed shifts yet, so a quick shower would help put some life back into her.

After she got out of the shower, she went over and kissed Andrew lightly on the cheek, and he stirred. "Honey, I didn't mean to wake you," and she sat down on the bed beside him to talk for a few minutes before getting dressed for work. He moved the head of the bed up to a sitting position and pulled her close to him. He brushed her robe from her shoulders and looked at her. Her nipples became hard, but when he pressed his mouth against them and took them in his mouth, her whole body trembled. He kissed her and whispered in her mouth, "You belong to me.".

Sharon was left breathless. "Oh, honey, please wait. What if someone comes in?" When he released her, she immediately stood. She was so discombobulated, she immediately went back to the bathroom and got back in the shower. Her heart was racing. Andrew had a way of touching her that was ever so gentle, but oh, so controlling, both at the same time. It was so unreal. Just minutes later, she heard the nurse talking. "Mr. Grayson, you're awake early. Is everything okay?"

"I'm looking for my wife," she heard Dru say in that low morning voice.

"I think she might be in the shower, but I can help you if you need anything," she heard the nurse say.

"No, I'm fine. Thanks."

"Okay," she said, "But please, Mr. Grayson, ring if

you need anything. Please don't try to get up on your own. Be sure and let us help you."

"That sounds like a warning," he said, and she laughed.

It took Sharon a while to pull herself together. She was a mess but in a good way. Dru was a drug to her, pulsating through her body, and she definitely was addicted. He had a unique way of using his senses to bring her to the full extent of pure passion. Touching: ever so gently, yet seductively all at the same time, demanding she gives into his control. Watching: never taking his eyes from hers, watching her passion build in intensity, using his sense of smell, drawing her in with each breath. Listening: listening to the sounds that pleasure makes. Tasting: tasting her with his kisses. His lips, his tongue, then talking to her with his deep throaty voice that makes her hot like a shot of adrenaline coursing through her body.

Andrew definitely knew how to use all of his senses meticulously, but there was something else Sharon noticed about him several times before that she thought was so unusual. He had an unnatural gift. The first time she was made aware of it was the day she fell and by the people who saw it with their own eyes because she was unconscious. The people who were there that day said that Anne literally carried her up this steep embankment and held her in his arms until help arrived. Everyone who was there that day talked about how another woman should not have been able to do that alone. It has been said that sometimes in life and death situations, people have gotten extra strength, but this was altogether different.

Then there was the night they made love. Sharon was so excited, but Andrew was in full control. He placed his hands on her hips and gently moved them around in a slow tantalizing grind, not too deep, but just deep enough, coordinating perfectly with the movement of his own body and knowing exactly when it was time to introduce them both to ultimate pleasure.

Also, there was the day in the shower. Andrew had already brought her to the point of no return. She rested her back against his chest and his arms encircled her, cupping her sex in his hands. "Let your body relax," he whispered. He never inserted a finger. The less he tampered with her, the better. With just the stroke of his hand rubbing against that special place, made her lose all control. She could feel it coming from way down deep inside her, and so could he. But with him, it was all about timing, timing and placement - the palm of his hand placed perfectly between her legs, his forearms gliding gently against the nipples of her breast – such balance, such form, such control, such pleasure. It was like being caught up in an erotic dance. When she was spent, he scooped her up in his arms, carried her to their bed, covered her, and whispered softly in her ear, "You rest."

20

Oh my, Sharon had lost all sense of time. When she finally pulled her head together and finished getting dressed, she left the bathroom and went over and stood beside Dru's bed, but she stayed her distance this time. He looked at her intensely. "Sharon, you're not upset with me, are you?" he asked quietly as she detected an air of uncertainty in his voice.

"Honey, you know I'm not," she assured him, and relief came over him. "I'm glad. I don't want to ever do anything you don't want me to," he said.

"Dru, I love you so much," and she leaned over and kissed him lightly on the lips. He looked at her not just seeing her physical beauty. "You are so beautiful, you know that? There is a pureness about you that I will never take away from you. I am so lucky to have a woman like you to love me," he said. "When I think about how I hurt you when I tried to drive you away, it causes me tremendous pain in my heart."

She could see the sorrow and the desperation in his eyes, and she spoke. "Dru, I was never going to let that happen. You are going to have to make me an honest woman, and I will see to it that you do." He beamed with pride. Tomorrow was their big day, and when she returned, they would spend the rest of the evening together making plans.

"Will you be back soon?" Andrew asked.

"Soon, honey," she promised and turned and left the room. She knew that was best because she could tell how much he wanted her to stay, but they had a wonderful three-day weekend together, and she could hardly wait.

"Good morning, ladies."

"Good morning, Dr. Robinson they all said

Louise, are you ready for your new adventure?"

"Yes, doctor, most definitely, and thank you and Sharon again for this wonderful opportunity." He assured her that she had earned it. "Your work performance and dedication to The Company and your own department over the years reflect that," and then he turned to Chrystal.

"Ms. Chrystal, you're in store for a tremendous learning opportunity as well. Use it to your advantage. I have a feeling it won't be too long before Anne gets back, but until then, I know that the three of you will be fine.

"A few weeks ago, I gave Sharon a special assignment to work on that has proven to be a tremendous success. She decided to step out of her comfort zone and use her own creative style and grace as the perfect platform to market our latest trends in women's fashions and accessories. Through her social media site, people who knew her by The Company she keeps, no pun intended, actually did the work for her. People like doing business with someone they already know, relate to, and trust, and that's Sharon. Do you see where I'm coming from ladies? With the rapport she has established with her followers, they know what we were all about and that's quality and trust. Our sales have tripled in the last ninety days. You ladies understand what makes you look and feel good, and that's ultimately what sells."

"And Sharon already knew that, though," Louise added.

"My point exactly, Louise. Through her blog and her own look and style, it helps women create their own unique styles as well. They tell her what they would like to see, their likes and dislikes, but most of all, she creates an unbreakable bond with this company. There's nothing like word of mouth. So, ladies, get your creative juices flowing and set this company on the map. It goes without saying, but if there is anything you need or any ideas you would like to share and/or implement, just let me know. Holistic Medicine is my baby," he said proudly, "But the door is wide open for advancement in The Company. Soon I will have no choice but to start the interviewing process or maybe have a job fair. Long-term employees like Anne are already stockholders and have been here for at least ten years of service. Ladies, I'm not going to hold you up any longer. Go out and enjoy your lunch break and Sharon, I will see you on Monday."

"Thank you, Dr. Robinson," they all chimed in together.

After he left the office, they all took a deep breath. "Boy, that was an eye opener of a meeting," Louise said.

"Yes, it was," Sharon had to agree. "He left a lot for us to take in, didn't he?"

At this point, Chrystal decided to say something. She had been quiet the whole time. "No wonder when Anne got this job, she stayed put. She should be loaded by now." They laughed so hard. When Lou caught her breath, she thought about it again and asked, "Chrystal, what are you talking about?"

"I'm talking about Anne. Look at how long she's been a stockholder at The Company. She should be loaded by now. Maybe I'll just hang around a little longer," she said. "Maybe even to retirement."

Sharon and Louise locked arms with Chrystal, one on each side. "Chrystal, for now, let's just go to lunch," and they all laughed.

"How about Houston's, my treat," Sharon suggested. "I'll even drive.

"I'm glad it's your treat, Chrystal said. "I'll even sit in the back." For sure, she was on a roll today.

After they placed their orders, they started brainstorming, and throwing different ideas out to each other. They discussed their likes and dislikes of different styles and fabrics.

Lou even reminded them that they even had a lot of men that liked to shop from the Company for the women in their lives as well.

"Lou, you are so right," Sharon agreed. "Now it will be so much easier for them to select something they know that a special woman will like and with personalized attention, too."

"Ladies, we're on the money today," Lou said excitedly.

Suddenly, Chrystal spotted Sharon's ring. "Oh, my goodness! Sharon, where in heaven's name did you get that beautiful ring?" Chrystal actually stood up and reached across the table and took Sharon by the hand. "Damn, girl.

Look, Lou, have you seen this?" she asked, stammering over her words. Sharon was not prepared. It had become a part of her and taking it off her finger was not an option.

"Look, Lou," Chrystal said again. Louise looked at Sharon quizzically and repositioned herself in her seat. Finally, Sharon said, "Anne gave it to me for my birthday. Isn't it the most beautiful thing you've ever seen?"

"Damn, Sharon, I guess. I bet that set Anne back a pretty penny."

"Well, I think I'm worth it," Sharon said, and she attempted to laugh it off, but Chrystal persisted.

"Look, Lou," she said for the third time. Lou decided to speak up and said, "I know, doesn't it just take your breath away? Those two stones complement each other beautifully, don't they? The emerald is Sharon's birthstone, and the diamond is a chocolate diamond."

"I already know that," Chrystal said with a slight sarcastic tone in her voice. "Anne definitely has class," Chrystal said. "I'll bet she had to cash in some of her stock for that."

The waiter's timing couldn't have been better when he came with their orders.

"Boy this looks great," Sharon said, trying to change the subject. "What did you order, Chrystal?"

"The seafood platter."

"I forgot they had that. I love seafood," Sharon said.

"Lou, your ribs look awesome."

"We'll all be ready for a nap after this," Lou said, and with that, she started talking about their future plans at The Company. Overall, the afternoon was fun, but Sharon knew that Chrystal was wondering why Anne would give her such a personal gift but she would just have to deal with that later.

They were quiet most of the drive back, until Sharon asked Louise if she knew when she would be officially transferring broke the silence.

Louise was pretty sure it wouldn't be this Monday, "she said. More like the following Monday.

"They will be interviewing this week and making a final decision on Friday. I will be glad when you do start," Sharon continued.

Girl, so do I! This is going to be an exciting time for all of us, Lou said. She could just feel it and they all agreed. When Sharon pulled up in front of Lou's building. "She thanked Sharon.

Sharon, thank you so much for a wonderful afternoon! This has been the perfect ending to the most perfect day "now if I can just manage not to sit at my desk and nod off and they all laughed.

When Sharon and Chrystal got back to the studio, Chrystal immediately spoke. "This has been so great Sharon, "thanks.

You got that right, Sharon agreed. "Today was fun, wasn't it Chrystal? " Trying to lift that feeling of awkwardness that seemed to manifest itself when it was just the two of them.

"Yes, it has Sharon, and thank you so much for the wonderful lunch.

This is going to be an exciting time for all of us, and I'm really looking forward to it as well. Chrystal replied.

Sharon could tell that Chrystal had a lot more on her mind than she was saying. So, she excused herself by saying she was going to her office to tie up some loose ends before leaving for the day since she would not be there tomorrow. "Have a great weekend, Chrystal, and I will see you bright and early Monday morning."

"You too, Sharon," she acknowledged, "And tell Anne I asked about her. "I was just thinking," she said as an afterthought, "I haven't been up to see Anne since she's been in the hospital. She probably thinks I don't care about her. I wanted to give her the chance to start feeling better before I went up and gave her a hard time," and then she kind of laughed it off.

"She would love it, Chrystal," Sharon said.

"I know," she agreed.

"Boy, that lunch is really weighing me down," Chrystal continued. "Maybe I will stay out just a little longer and try to shake this stuffy feeling, but if I don't see you before you leave, have a great weekend, Sharon."

"You too, Chrystal."

When Sharon got to her office, she collapsed in her chair. She was mentally exhausted. Things seemed to be piling up on her, and it bothered her not having better control. She realized how much she had begun to lean on Dru for mental support without even being aware of it. It was so strange, but now was definitely not the time for her to go soft. She had to keep it together and stay strong for the both of them.

Chrystal liked pushing Sharon's buttons, and that didn't help. It was probably due to Chrystal suspecting something was going on with Anne, but she didn't know what yet. Lately, she had been hanging on to Sharon's every word, especially if it had anything to do with Anne.

Sharon sat there for a minute trying to get it together, but she knew she was not going to get much done. She could only hope that she would be able to shake some of the emotional anxiety before she got to the hospital. She checked with Chrystal before leaving to make sure she didn't need anything.

She urgently needed to grocery shop and stock the fridge and do so many other things. With Dru coming home tomorrow and nothing organized, she felt inadequate, and she was not used to that feeling.

Before Anne and Sharon realized what was happening between them, she lived and breathed all the attention she got from her position at The Company, and for the most part, she still did. But with Anne's mother, the shooting, and everything else that happened over the last few weeks, it had left her shaken and uncertain.

"Hey, Ms. Pretty." Sharon could still hear Geraldine's sarcastic and deprecating tone, and it left Sharon not wanting to be viewed that way anymore, especially by someone like Geraldine Peterson. Geraldine Peterson was truly ugly on the inside and out. Her existence in their lives for that brief time had done so much damage and caused so much pain. Just knowing that people like her exist in the world and some even worse scared Sharon to death. After meeting Geraldine Peterson, Sharon realized that she had been viewing life through rose-colored glasses, and maybe it was time for her to take them off.

When Sharon went back out to Chrystal's desk, she still wasn't back yet, but it was no big deal. Things wouldn't be hopping until Monday anyway.

Sharon heard her phone ringing. She hoped no one needed anything pressing this late in the day.

"Sharon Grayson, may I help you?"

"Hi, Honey." It was Nanna. "Nanna, how are you?"

"Great, now that Andrew is doing so much better. I tried to call your cell, but it went to voicemail," she lamented.

"Oh, I'm sorry about that Nanna, but isn't it great how things are going with Andrew?"

"Yes honey, it is. I went to see him this morning,"

she continued, "And I can see how much he has progressed. The reason I am calling is because Andrew told me he is being released tomorrow. He is so excited. Are you going to be able to take tomorrow off?" she asked with anticipation in her voice.

"Yes. Dr. Robinson wouldn't have it any other way."

"That sounds like Benjamin," she said.

It was nice to hear Nanna call Dr. Robinson by his first name. They had been close high school friends and stayed close all these years.

"I'll be leaving here soon because I have so much to do before going to the hospital," Sharon offered.

"Well honey, that's why I called. "I started to surprise you, but I figured I'd better fess up. I have already gone grocery shopping for you and completely stocked up the cottage. You have enough food and supplies to last at least a month."

"Oh, my God, Nanna, you're not serious!"

"I'm as serious as a heart attack," and she chuckled.

Sharon couldn't help herself; tears began to flow. "Nanna, that's exactly what I was planning to do," she managed to say between the emotions and tears that were choking her up. "Nanna, can you imagine how overwhelmed I've been feeling just thinking about all of that?"

"Yes, I can, Sharon. That's why I thought I'd better

tell you. Heaven forbid that you do all that running around unnecessarily."

"Nanna, I love you so much."

"I know you do honey," she said. "Now try to relax this weekend and enjoy being together. By the way, the cottage looks beautiful. It reflects the both of you so well. Take care, honey, and if there is anything else I can do, just let me know, Okay, honey?"

Sharon told her that she would.

"Please stop crying honey, or you're going to make me cry," Nanna said softly. "We'll talk again soon."

After Sharon hung up the phone, she sobbed. She had to get all those pent-up emotions out of her body and mind. Chrystal, work, and all the rest of the negative thoughts that were weighing her down had to leave. Nanna's thoughtfulness today was a Godsend, literally speaking. That's the way people like Nanna are. The only thing she didn't have was something appropriate to sleep in at the hospital. She made a mad dash to the mall and was out in thirty minutes.

BOOK TITLE

21

When Sharon stepped off of the elevator, the clock said 4:30 p.m. Andrew would be so happy to see her. She was there much earlier than she normally would have been. When she got to the nurse's station, she stopped to chat like she always did and to make sure things were still a go for tomorrow's big day.

"Yes, he's good. He seems a little apprehensive, plus he's had a lot of visitors today. Your Nanna was here first thing this morning, and that always sets his day. He enjoys her visits very much, but with physical therapy and last-minute things to be done, it was probably overwhelming to him," the nurse reported.

"I can imagine," Sharon acknowledged.

The nurse paused for a moment, and when they were alone, she spoke. "Mrs. Grayson, Mr. Grayson's last visitor was here quite a while, and I noticed a tremendous change in his mood when she left. I'm surprised you didn't see her on your way up."

"It was a woman? Did she give her name?"

"No, but when she came up, she asked for Anne. At first, I thought she meant Andrew, but when she said Peterson, that threw up a red flag."

Sharon immediately knew. "I thought you should know about this, and felt I could talk to you in confidence," the nurse explained.

"You know you can," Sharon assured her. "I have a gut feeling I already know who she is, a nosey coworker," Sharon grumbled. Sharon thanked her for telling her about this and appreciated her and the rest of the nurses for being so supportive of Andrew and her as well. Sharon assured her that this conversation would stay between them.

"Thank you, Mrs. Grayson." Sharon asked her if she and Andrew could have a little quiet time after she went in. "Of course, Mrs. Grayson. I will make sure you are not disturbed," and Sharon thanked her again for everything.

Sharon peeked her head in the door and said, "Hi honey, I'm all yours." He smiled widely.

"I'm glad, and I wish we could leave right now."

"What difference will a few more hours make?". Sharon smiled. She was not about to step into his trap. "Has Dr. Clarke given you a time tomorrow?" she asked.

"Not exactly. The massage therapist Dr. Robinson hired for me will be coming at 11:00 a.m., and this will be the last thing I will have to do. Once that's over, we can blow this joint." The excitement was almost more than they could contain.

She started to pull up a chair beside him, but he said, "No honey, come and sit in the chair with me. It's big enough for both of us," he said grinning. "I'll play nice, I promise." Sharon felt her face flush.

"Promises, promises," she said. She took her shoes off and snuggled down in the chair beside him, entwining their bodies together. It felt wonderful. They sat quietly together for a long time, and for a while, she thought he had fallen asleep.

"Sharon, Chrystal was here today." Sharon did not acknowledge that she already knew. "She stayed for a while." He continued, "You don't have to be careful or watch what you say or how you act around her anymore."

"Dru what happened?" Sharon asked.

"I told Chrystal the truth. It was time, Sharon. Over half of The Company has their suspicions, and in this day and age, how many really care?" When Andrew said that Sharon was shocked. Andrew went on, "There is no way we will be able to comfortably work together until I took a stand. She talked about you guys going out to lunch together today and how beautiful your ring is.

"Oh honey, I'm sorry about that," Sharon immediately replied. "I knew I should not have kept it on, but Dru, when you placed the ring on my finger, I knew I would never want to take it off."

"Sharon, you don't have to say sorry about anything. Our love for each other has been tested to its limits, and I'm tired of it. It's time for me to come out of the closet, so to speak." He sat quietly again for what seemed like eternity as if to relish the clarity in his spirit and heart that had finally given him peace. Finally, he said, "You know the irony of all of this? The one and only good thing my mother ever did for me was to expose me for the freak of nature she conceived."

"Andrew, please don't say that." She could hardly speak because she was so overcome.

"Sharon, I'm finally the man I was destined to be from the moment you told me you loved me. For so many years, my mother robbed me of any identity at all. By forcing me to live as someone she knew I was not, left me an empty shell all because nature decided to give me both. What is it about me that would allow something so barbaric to go on all of my adult life and not retaliate? That's the part that is so hard for me to explain, even to myself. Even after I escaped her poisonous venom, she was still able to keep me debilitated."

Sharon had never seen Andrew like this before, and it scared her. "I told Chrystal that I was in love with you, and the ring I gave you was a birthday gift and an engagement ring, and the final decision was left up to you. The longer you keep it on your finger, the better my chances are, but no matter the outcome, my love for you will never go away. Now Chrystal knows the truth, and it came straight from the horse's mouth. I asked her to no longer call me Anne. I informed her that I have legally changed my name to Andrew Grayson. I told her that you graciously offered me your last name, and I accepted it. Sharon, do you know what Chrystal had the nerve to say? She asked me if Dr. Robinson knew about all of this."

"What?" Sharon almost yelled.

"Yep, but you know what honey, I never lost my

composure. I refreshed her memory by asking her about the day all this happened. Was she present or not? I asked her if she had to submit a written statement just like everyone else did."

"Dru, what did she say?" Sharon inquired. Dru responded with a resolute, "Nothing." "I told her the one thing I am not is a fool, and as far as changing my name is concerned, Dr. Robinson knows and gave me his blessing. I let her know my name change has legally gone through the court system, and when I return to work, there will be no secrets." The big secret was finally out, and it felt so good.

"Honey, I believe Chrystal has always known how I feel about you for quite a while now," Sharon said. "The fact that I am still wearing your ring confirms it." They sat there together enjoying the closeness of their bodies touching. Andrew had pretty much said everything that needed to be said, and they both took a deep breath and sighed a big sigh of relief.

About 7:00 p.m., they heard a gentle knock on the door. The nurse apologized for disturbing them. She was there to give Andrew his nighttime meds and see if he was ready to lay down. "No problem," they both said. "Both of us are ready to turn in early because we have a big rest of our lives to get on with, and we can hardly wait," and Sharon could not have said it better.

While Dru was getting settled for the evening, Sharon went into the bathroom to freshen up and change her clothes. She noticed she had a message from Louise.

"Hey, girl! Have a great weekend with Andrew, and I want to give you some good news. I will be doing half days up there with you starting Monday until they hire someone for my position."

"Oh, my goodness Lou," Sharon said out loud. This made things so much better. Now she wouldn't have to spend Monday morning alone with Chrystal. Sharon quickly texted back. "Oh Lou, you have no idea how happy this news makes me. You won't believe how much I have to tell you. We'll talk over the weekend. Love you, Lou."

Sharon couldn't believe how strange things had been today. Help had always come when she felt the most helpless. She felt blessed to have people in her and Dru's life who only wanted the best for them. They always seemed to know when they needed their support and stepped up when they least expected it.

When Sharon went back into the room, Dru was already sleeping, and she was glad. He could finally feel free. Tomorrow would be another busy day for them, but because of their close circle of friends, it would be wonderful.

Sharon had a hard time falling asleep. Chrystal was going to be trouble, she could feel it, but before she prejudged her, she could at least give her the benefit of the doubt. Maybe all she really wanted was to feel truly accepted and no longer an outsider, but Sharon had a strong inkling that wasn't the case at all. All she had to say was, "Sharon, I think I'll go up and spend some time with Anne." The door was wide open for her to do that earlier, but she preferred to be sneaky and maybe catch Anne off guard, and ultimately, things backfired. She understood what Chrystal was all about, but Chrystal really didn't want to get on Sharon's bad side when it came to Dru.

When the massage therapist came in after breakfast, that would give Sharon the opportunity to call and talk to Louise. She knew she wouldn't mind her calling so early.

"Good morning, Mrs. Grayson. You're up bright and early," the nurse said. "Well, I am up," Sharon agreed, "but ready I'm not so sure of. When we get home, we are going to hibernate all weekend."

"I can't blame you one bit," the nurse said. "You can probably use the break. You have a very hectic schedule as well."

"We both do," Sharon agreed. "We can't begin to express to all of you how special you have become to Andrew and me. We've come a long way from that night so many weeks ago, and we could never truly express how grateful we are to have you on this journey with us," Sharon stressed.

"Mrs. Grayson, thank you so much for saying that to us," the two attendants said. "It's people like you that keep us dedicated to why we're here, and it's days like today that make this journey worthwhile."

"Can't a man get some sleep around here?" Andrew woke up and spoke. All anyone could do was laugh.

Sharon went over and sat down on the bed beside

him. "It's time for you to wake up anyway sleepy head. It's just about time for us to blow this joint."

He looked at her and gave her a sleepy smile. Andrew was so sexy to Sharon.

The nurse told them that the massage therapist would be there around 9:00 a.m., and that they would be able to order breakfast after that if that was okay with them. "No one wants to be pushed, punched, and stretched on a full stomach," they totally agreed. "Just relax Mr. Grayson, and we will come and get you when the therapist arrives," and Dru thanked them.

"Good morning, Mr. Grayson. Sharon leaned over and brushed her lips lightly against his face. Are you ready to go home?" He smiled. "So ready, honey." Sharon kissed him lightly on the lips and ran her fingers through his hair. Dru had changed so much. Maybe it was the way his body was built. Not muscular, but sexy and lean. All those years when no one knew he was really a man, even then Sharon found herself attracted to him, but watching him now, the way he moved, the confidence he felt about himself at this point, was so attractive.

Sharon held out her hand to him when he got up to walk to the shower, and she could feel his control, his true sense of self. The feel of his hand in the small of her back made her feel so connected to him. He even looked different. "Honey, I'll be okay," he said. "They have those bars in the shower for me to hold onto. I'll be out in a sec." The warmest feeling came over Sharon watching him move.

When he came out of the shower with his PJ bottoms and a T-shirt on, you could see the definition in his body. She could almost feel its hardness pressed against her naked body. Just the thought made her face feel flushed.

"Sharon honey, are you okay?" he asked.

"Yes, Dru, better than okay. Later I will show you just how much better." She stood on her tippy toes and let her body surrender to his embrace. He wrapped his arms around her waist and pressed her close to him. "Mrs. Grayson, you wouldn't be coming on to me, would you?" he asked in his deep throaty voice.

Just at that moment, the nurse walked in and brought them back to reality. "They're ready for you in P.T., Mr. Grayson." He took a step back from Sharon, never taking his eyes off of hers. "Would you like for us to take you down in a wheelchair?"

"No, that's okay. I'm just a little slow right now, but I would prefer to walk down."

"Cool," she said. "I have all the time in the world. We do twelve hour shifts here," she said, and Dru couldn't help but laugh. Sharon told him she was going to run a few errands, but she would be back by the time he was finished.

"I'll be ready," he said. "See you soon."

After they left, Sharon went down to one of the family waiting rooms and called Louise. She answered on the second ring.

Sharon apologized for calling so early, but she had to tell her about what happened last evening. "No worries, girl," she said. "I have been awake for a while just lying here. What's up? I got your text last night," she said. "I was hoping you would get a chance to call."

"Louise, Dru had a visitor yesterday after we came back from lunch. Guess who?"

"Chrystal."

"You guessed it. Lou, instead of her just coming out and telling me that she would make a quick trip to the hospital to see Andrew before he was released, not that she needs my permission, she lied. She had every intention of going up to the hospital and putting Dru on the hotseat about the ring, but actually Lou, she got way more than she bargained for."

"Why, what happened?"

"When she finally got in to see Dru, he told her the whole story."

"What? You're not serious!"

"Lou, he said it was time for him to start accepting responsibility for himself, and he was not going to sit back and watch Chrystal play little mind games that seemed to give her so much pleasure when it came to him. He knows Chrystal likes pushing my buttons, and he is tired of it. Lou, you know that Chrystal was there the day Andrew's mother was saying all of that terrible stuff about Dru, and anyone with a computer can find out what his condition means.

Chrystal is a piece of work and then some. When I got up to Andrew's floor yesterday, the charge nurse stopped me and told me about a visitor Dru had who had just left. She told me the woman was asking for Anne Peterson, and that's what threw up a red flag. When Dru heard her out at the nurse's station, he came to the door. Lou, excuse my French, but Chrystal Johnson is a piece of shit. Andrew told her that when he came back to work, he would appreciate it if she no longer called him Anne Peterson, and that he had legally changed his name to Andrew. He told her that I had graciously shared my last name with him, and he accepted, and that Andrew Grayson was now his legal name. Dru also told her he was in love with me Louise, and the ring was a birthday present as well as an engagement ring. He let her know that as long as I keep it on my finger, it lets him know that I care about him as well. Lou, do you know what Chrystal had the nerve to say?"

"I'm afraid to ask," Louise said.

"And I quote, 'Does Dr. Robinson know about all of this?'"

"Damn, Sharon, this is some real drama here." When Louise finally absorbed the ramifications of all of this, she asked, "Sharon, are you going to let Dr. Robinson know about what happened?"

"Nope. Chrystal doesn't know who she is dealing with, Lou. Have you heard that old saying that you can catch more flies with honey than with vinegar? Well, we shall see."

"Lord, Sharon, you can bet I'm wide awake now," Louise said, and both laughed. "This has been a real eye-opener because I can see there is more to Chrystal than meets the eye. Please don't let any of this ruin your weekend with Dru, please, sis. You two desperately need this time to reconnect."

"Oh, don't worry Lou," Sharon reassured her. "That's the last thing I'm going to let Chrystal do. In fact, I would be willing to bet that Chrystal is walking around on pins and needles right about now, worrying about the problem she has created for herself now that she knows the whole story."

"No Lou, the last thing I'm going to do is go running to Dr. Robinson with this. We have too much work to do. I'll leave that up to Chrystal to do it in her own dirty little sneaky way. And when she does, that will be her downfall. No one likes a shit stirrer, Lou, especially Dr. Robinson. See you bright and early Monday morning, and I love you, Lou."

By the time Sharon got back up to Andrew's room, he was coming down the hall still walking. The nurse said she tried to get him to let her push him back in a wheelchair, but he said he really needed to build his endurance. When the nurse wasn't looking, he looked at Sharon and winked. When they got back to the room, he laid down on the bed, and she sat down beside him. She could tell it had taken a lot out of him, and she let him rest. She asked him if he wanted dietary to send up something light until he got to Haven House, but he declined. All he wanted was her and to feel him inside her. Just thinking about it was driving him crazy, and just listening to him put it into words made her whole body hot.

Sharon tried to get the notion out of his head. "Dru honey, you know we should wait just a little longer and see what Dr. Clarke says." He didn't comment on that, and she knew that no matter what the doctor said, she would not be able to keep him away from her for very long. "When Dr. Clarke comes in, we'll see what his final instructions are, okay honey?"

"Okay Sharon, but if he doesn't mention it, neither are we. I want you so badly Sharon," and she knew he was serious.

"I promise that I won't ask anything about being intimate, but I don't want anything to go wrong either."

"It won't honey," and he smiled. She didn't say anything else, but she understood that once they got to Haven House, trying to resist him would be useless.

Dr. Clarke stuck his head in the door. "Are you decent?" Andrew immediately responded back. "Ask me when we get home." Sharon liked Dr. Clarke very much. He was down to earth.

"Well, I can't say I hate to see you leave because this day gave him so much joy."

"Thank you so much for everything, doctor," Andrew said. "I can't put into words how much you have meant to me and his recovery."

"You are quite welcome, Andrew."

"Now doc, when can I go back to work?" Dr. Clarke massaged his forehead like Dru had just given him an instant headache and mumbled something under his breath and smiled.

"Andrew, this is something I'm going to be dragging my feet on for a while. I want you to be off for at least a month."

"A month, doc?"

"Andrew, your injuries were critical. Someone higher up, together with my skills, are why you're still here today. I truly could not have done it alone, so I refuse to take any chances. Will you agree to work with me on this, Andrew?"

"You know I will, Dr. Clarke. Whatever you say."

"Thank you, Andrew, plus the massage therapist who will be coming out to see you starting Monday will be the best thing since sliced bread. So, use it for all it's worth. Heck, I'd love to have access to one of them at my disposal. Man, they're great," Dr. Clarke said. "Andrew, all I want the two of you to do is to reconnect with each other and get those wedding plans back in motion. I know I warrant an invitation."

"You betcha, Dr. Clarke," Sharon said.

"Andrew, you're free to go whenever you're ready, no rush. The nurses told me you walked all the way to PT and back today. Please allow them to take you down in a wheelchair while Sharon brings the car around. I want to see you the week before you go back to work, okay?"

"Thanks again, Dr Clarke, for everything you've done for Sharon and me," he said. "See you in a month." After he left, Dru said, "Let's go home honey." They held each other for a long time, and when Andrew got to the car, "Shining Star" was playing. That was one of his favorite CDs. Andrew loved music, and so did she.

22

When Sharon and Andrew turned off the highway into the drive leading to the cottage, it reminded her of the first time she ever shared it with Andrew. In fact, it was the first time she had ever shared it with anyone. That day seemed like such a long time ago now. So much had happened to them since then, but together they had survived. Sharon got out of the car and unlocked the door. She could tell Andrew was having some discomfort getting out of the car and he grimaced when he took the three steps leading up to the porch.

"Sharon, it feels great to be back here," and that feeling of healing radiated in his eyes. They had everything arranged pretty much the way it was at her old place, and they loved camping out on the floor between the sofas. It was their own little secret hideaway with the oversized pillows and the delightful covers from her bed.

She had Dru sit down and get comfortable while she

went to get his meds from the car. The sofa was inviting and comfortable. It had extra-large pillows across the back and plenty of space to rest the back. She fixed him a glass of iced tea and gave him his meds. "Come and sit beside me honey," he said. Sharon kicked off her shoes and curled up beside him on the sofa, and peace overtook them both.

It didn't take long at all for her to feel his body relax. He had his back pressed against the pillows and his head resting against her thigh. It was awesome to see him resting and not in pain. Now she could concentrate on dinner. Haven House had a way of fixing you when you were broken in body and spirit, and she knew it would do that for Dru.

She went into the kitchen to see what she could find to put together. Nanna was right. There wasn't too much left in the store when she finished shopping. Sharon decided on homemade cream of potato soup, and if she wanted it to taste anywhere as good as Dru's, she'd better get started because there was a lot of preparation, at least for her anyway. For Dru, it was a breeze.

She couldn't get over Chrystal. Women like Chrystal become really insecure when they have to deal with women like her, and that was sad because she would have done anything to help push her up. She wanted Chrystal to take advantage of the opportunities put in place for her just like Dr. Robinson said, and to accomplish any goal she put in place for herself. Women like Chrystal can be their own worst enemy. They will cut off their noses to spite their face as Nanna used to say. It's called envy. All Sharon could do was sit back and watch her self-destruct.

Dinner turned out better than Sharon hoped, if she had to say so herself.

"Hey, Mrs. Grayson, what are you brewing up in there? I'm starved."

"Your timing is perfect," Sharon responded back. "I made homemade cream of potato soup just like you showed me with bacon, real butter and cream. It turned out great. It's ready whenever you are."

"As soon as I take a quick shower to take the stiffness out, I will be ready, and thanks, honey."

Sharon heard the shower running, and she wanted to join him but decided against it. She would know when the time was right, and now wasn't the right time. When Andrew came back carrying the delightful covers from their bed, he said, "Guess where we're sleeping tonight?" They both looked at each other and giggled.

"Okay, you fix that while I fix the trays," she said. He moved all of the pillows from the sofa onto the floor. After dinner, Dru suggested having a movie night. Remembering that she was a horror movie buff. "You pick," he said. Sharon could tell the night was going to be special and she headed to the shower.

After she came out of the shower, Dru told her the soup was really good. "Hospital food can leave you with a bad taste in your mouth, if you know what I mean," he said. She knew exactly what he meant because she had shared many meals with him at the hospital these past few weeks. After dinner, the first thing Dru wanted to talk about was getting their wedding plans back on track. "Dr. Clarke was right honey, and the sooner the better," and Sharon agreed.

"While you were in the shower, I came up with a wonderful idea. Can I run it by you?" he asked excitedly.

"Sure honey, I'm listening."

"June is right around the corner. What does that bring to mind?" She thought for a moment. "Well, vacations, summer weddings, bridal showers, the works," and then it hit her. "Andrew, our wedding would make the perfect platform for my blog."

"Honey, do you know what that would mean for The Company, plus it would be something we could work on together until you come back to work?" They were exuberant over the idea.

"Sharon, this will be great," he said. "I won't feel so unproductive while you're gone during the day. Let's brainstorm and come up with some creative ways to gain followers. With the new fashion line coming out this summer, now would be the perfect time to announce our engagement and start a perfect bride contest," he said. "Every week, when someone places an order of fifty dollars or more, they can submit a copy of their favorite summer bride photo. Every week a photo will be selected and put into a drawing. At the end of the contest, a final winner will be selected for an eight-day, all-inclusive cruise to the Bahamas," he suggested.

"Damn Honey, where is that coming from?"

"From Dr. Robinson, of course, but take a look at what this could do for The Company. We would make The Company one of the top runners in public relations with social media as a marketing tool."

"Dru, this could be a win-win," she replied.

Drew resumed, "It would give our customers the ideal venue to share their stories about their special day, submit photos of the bride and groom, and provide an authentic way to make them feel like a part of what The Company is all about and that's customer satisfaction. Sharon, you have a unique style that has captured your media followers, and that's what's going to make this promotion so successful. You have a natural feminine side, but it also lets them see that it exists in all women. All they need to do is be themselves and let it shine through. Sharon, we will be the power couple behind The Company," he concluded.

"Dru, you connect really well with the men in our lives, especially those who are looking for that special piece for that special woman. That makes you the icing on the cake, Dru," and he smiled. They were so excited about this promotion, they lost all track of time, and when they looked at the clock, it was after midnight. It was like watching Dru be born again.

Sharon knew that Dr. Clarke said he would have to be off for a month, and now, there would be no reason why he could not work from home. "I will talk to Dr. Robinson Monday and ask him if the four of us can get together on a conference call. This is your idea Dru," Sharon told him,

"And you should be the one to present it to the group. In fact, I will leave a little earlier on Monday so I can stop and talk to Dr, Robinson."

"Sharon, I don't know about that," he said, his excitement beginning to fade. "Do you really think Dr. Robinson would?"

"Honey, Dr. Robinson has already told us to start brainstorming, and that includes you as well, Dru. I bet this contribution of yours is going to drop kick sales as well as recognition right out of the park."

He smiled. "I love you so much, Mrs. Grayson."

"I love you more," she said and touched his face. Finally, she said, "Honey, it's past time for us to get some rest, but do you really think us sleeping on the floor was a good idea for you? Maybe we should get in the bed so you can rest your back better," and he agreed. They grabbed the covers, and the rest they would do tomorrow. At last, life felt good.

Sharon wasn't looking forward to the weekend ending, but she could hardly wait to talk to Dr. Robinson about Andrew's idea. She knew that currently, things were only in the planning stages, but she could see such potential. When she woke up the next morning, Andrew was already up. He was outside on the steps doing toning exercises. The steps seemed to bother him yesterday, and he was determined to work through it, but she didn't want him to overdo it. "Dru, please be careful," is all she would say.

"Hi Honey. What are you doing up so early?" he

asked and smiled.

"Probably the same reason you are," and he laughed softly. "When you illuminate the full scope of this promotion Dru, the sky is the limit." She knew they couldn't get their hopes up until Dr. Robinson gave them his blessing, but Sharon was certain that once Andrew presented it to him, he would feel the same way.

By the end of the weekend, they had some wonderful ideas for the contest rules. They didn't want to make it complicated, just fun and exciting, but Andrew was a true perfectionist and every aspect had to be just so. Neither of them hardly slept at all, and first thing, Monday morning, Sharon was up and ready for the day. With Louise working with her today from 8:00 a.m. until 11:00 p.m., this would make for a whirlwind of a day.

Dru had a very busy day as well with therapy, which was a good thing because he was a bundle of nerves, and if things went the way they hoped, this project would be just like him being back to work. She went over beside him and took his hand and asked him how he was feeling after his first full day back home.

"Mentally, I feel great," he said. "But physically, my body isn't connecting as well as I would like for it to." She could hear the concern in his voice. She reminded him that was probably why Dr. Clarke was not ready for him to physically come back to work, and she repeated that technically, he would still be working. That brought a smile to his face.

"Your therapist comes at 11:00," she continued, "And after Dr. Robinson gives the okay for the conference call, you will be able to get some well-needed rest."

"I wish I felt as confident as you do," he said. Sharon hated to see him like this, physically not one hundred percent and uncertain about his position at work as well. Sharon assured him that he should be hearing something from her within the hour. "Please try to relax, honey."

Even though she knew this was a win for The Company, she still was anxious. More than anything else, she wanted a positive outcome for Dru. When she pulled up in the parking lot and saw Dr. Robinson's car, she breathed a sigh of relief. This was a big day for all of them but for Andrew most of all.

"Good morning, Sharon, how are you this beautiful morning?" the receptionist greeted.

"Great Marie, and how are you?"

Dr. Robinson heard her. "Sharon is that you so bright and early?"

"Yes, doctor. How are you this morning?" He gave her a huge belly laugh.

"Did Louise tell you the good news?" he asked.

"Yes, she did. She texted me on Friday just as we were leaving the hospital, and that made for the perfect weekend for Andrew and I."

"How was he when you left this morning?" he

asked.

"Well, right now anxious, which gets me to the reason I'm here. Dr. Robinson, Andrew has come up with a summer promotion that he urgently wants you to hear. Even though Dr. Clarke said he cannot come back to work for another month, there is no reason why he should not be able to work from home. Do you think that sometime this morning, the four of us could get together on a conference call, and he could do a presentation to all of us together?" Sharon could see a light come on in Dr. Robinson's eyes.

"I should have known that the two of you would come up with creative ways to still do great things. That's why you have become such a valuable asset to The Company in these few short years. You have a way of bringing out the best in others as well. Your qualities are rare, Sharon. In fact, around 11:00, I will get Andrew on the line first and then connect with you three ladies. We can all hear it together."

Sharon felt like her heart would burst, she was so excited. "Dr. Robinson, thank you so much for everything, and you will not be disappointed. Talk to you soon."

23

When Sharon got out to her car, she felt like she was hyperventilating, she was so excited. She couldn't do anything at that moment but sit there and try to get a second wind. She took deep breaths and called Andrew. He answered on the first ring.

"Sharon?" he answered.

"It's a go, honey."

"What?"

"You heard me right," she said. Dr. Robinson will be calling you at 11:00, and then he will bring the three of us in on the conference call."

"Sharon, I'm so nervous," he said.

"Honey, just take a few deep breaths, relax and wait for Dr. Robinson's call."

"I love you Sharon," he said, and then he hung up.

This day had already started off with a bang, but the real fireworks were yet to begin. "Good morning, Chrystal."

"Hello," she sheepishly replied. Louise came out of the conference room when she heard Sharon's voice.

"Surprise."

"Surprise is right," Sharon said and hugged her. "I received your message over the weekend, and I'm so glad. We'll take what we can get until we can get you full time, won't we Chrystal?" They gathered around Chrystal's desk and chatted like her little visit to Andrew never happened.

Louise seemed pretty much at a loss, just like Chrystal, and when Chrystal's phone rang, that temporarily lifted the strain of the situation. "Good morning, Chrystal Johnson, may I help you? Dr. Robinson, good morning," She paused. "Yes, she is, just one moment please. Sharon, it's Dr. Robinson, he wants to speak with you."

"Good morning, Doctor. Yes, I know that. Thank you, Dr. Robinson, we will be waiting. Ladies, it appears Dr. Robinson has some ideas he would like to run by us this morning before getting our day started, so let's grab our notepads and take good notes." Chrystal seemed relieved at the change of events and breathed a silent sigh of relief.

"Louise, would you please grab a couple of notepads

and pens from my office?" Sharon asked, "And we can sit in the conference room." Sharon quickly grabbed a cup of coffee and by the time she got back, the conference room phone was ringing. Sharon picked up the receiver.

"Ladies, good morning," came Dr. Robinson's cheery voice.

"Good morning, doctor," they said in unison. "I've got someone who wants to talk to you this morning." Sharon's heart was pounding in her chest. "Louise, Chrystal, Sharon, good morning. I miss you guys," he said.

"It's Andrew," Louise said. "We miss you too."

"Chrystal, are you there as well?"

"Yes," she said, her voice slightly cracking.

"Are you home yet," she asked?

"Yes, finally, and it feels good to be back. I figured just because Dr. Clarke is trying to hold me hostage doesn't mean I can't contribute from home, and Dr. Robinson has agreed to listen to some ideas I've been rolling around in my head. I would like it if you would give me some feedback. Okay, here I go."

"Through Sharon's blog, when we think of summer, we think of weddings, June brides, bridal showers and being in love. So, I thought by announcing to her followers that she is engaged, this would be the ideal platform to promote the perfect bride contest. When they visit the site, it will say, 'The Company – We are defined by the company we keep'.

Then Sharon will say, 'Guess who's engaged? You guessed it. Your very own Sharon Grayson and her creative consultant, Andrew Grayson, and no, it's not a misquote. We actually have the same last name. Now, how perfect is that? I won't even have to change my name when I marry him. So, let's celebrate. Every week, we will select, and feature photos submitted by you of your perfect day, and every week a photo will be drawn at random and placed in a final drawing to take place on August 5th. The winner will win an all-inclusive eight-day, all expenses paid honeymoon cruise to the Bahamas. So, ladies, start submitting your photos of your most special day.' I have decided to invite all of our May brides as well because May is our engagement month and my birthday. I'm wanting to spread the love. Every time you direct a friend, relative, or even yourself and place an order of fifty dollars or more, it puts your photos in the drawing for the trip. It's a different spin on a bridal registry. When your guests purchase your gifts from The Company, it will again place your photos in the drawing several more times, so be sure and tell them that your bridal registry is at The Company. You can also visit Andrew and I every day through my blog and get further instructions as they become available.'"

When Andrew finished with his presentation, Sharon was in awe. Dru asked Dr. Robinson first what he thought, but Dr. Robinson wanted to save his comments for last, so Louise spoke up immediately. "Dru, not that I am partial, but if handled correctly, this could send our sales through the roof, especially using The Company blog as a bridal registry. What a unique idea."

"Thank you, Lou," Andrew said. Dr. Robinson spoke up. "Why are you so quiet, Sharon?" he joked. "Do you think Andrew may be stepping on your toes?" Everyone laughed.

"Dr. Robinson, you might be right," she said and laughed as well.

Finally, Chrystal spoke up. "Yeah, it would be a great concept coming from someone else. I don't think Andrew and Sharon should be working so closely together considering all the negative publicity we're just beginning to get because of the shooting."

The silence was deafening, and Sharon wanted to jump up and start screaming. At this, Dr. Robinson directed his comments directly to Chrystal. "Chrystal, number one, Andrew Grayson has no significance to Sharon's followers at all; and number two, Sharon Grayson is someone her followers' trust. They see Andrew Grayson and Sharon Grayson as a power couple doing great things together just like they are doing in their personal lives. So, Chrystal, what are you basing your concerns on?" She didn't respond. Dr. Robinson went on, "Let me just say that these two people are in love just like their followers are, and sometimes Chrystal, love can hide a multitude of faults." Dr. Robinson expanded his thoughts. "Andrew, I think that the two of you are a perfect fit collaborating together on Sharon's blog. It will be a convenient and simple way for men to shop and get ideas for that special woman in their lives as well as shop for themselves. Andrew, I am so proud of you," he said. "You have been through so much. Welcome home and keep up the good work. Oh, and by the way, your new name reflects the true warrior that you are, and before I end this call, I will leave the four of you with this thought: Anne Marie Peterson doesn't exist anymore!"

After Dr. Robinson disconnected from the call, they all sat there mulling over the challenges that lay ahead for them these next few weeks and then, Sharon spoke up. "Well ladies, Andrew is definitely going to be making up for lost time, wouldn't you agree?" Lou laughed softly and said, "You got that right, Sharon." Chrystal said nothing.

"Well Lou, let's first start by checking out your office. We can share mine," Sharon said, "Better yet, you can always camp out in Dru's office until he comes back and kicks you out."

"You got that right, because at the rate he's going I'll be kicked out of there before this month is over," Lou said. The rest of the morning was business as usual. When they got to Sharon's office, Louise looked at Sharon completely bewildered. "Strike one," Sharon said and left it at that.

The word, perfect, didn't seem to express how Sharon felt about how the day had been thus far. She wanted to call Andrew so badly. Therapy should have been close to being over by now, and she hoped he would rest until she got home, but knowing Andrew, he wouldn't. Lou left at 12:30 p.m. so she could grab some lunch before going back to her own duties by 1:00. The rest of the day seemed to drag.

Sharon put in a call to engineering to get some furniture moved around and to decide where her office would eventually wind up. She didn't mind sharing her office with Lou, but sometimes it's nice to have a quiet place of your own to escape to. Engineering said they would be able to do it Friday, and that was fine since Lou would not be officially coming down until next week.

At last, she decided to go to lunch, mostly to make the time go by faster. She was so bored, and when she went up front to let Chrystal know, she was already gone. No problem, she thought to herself, she would be back soon. She went back to her office and tried to get a jump on things because after she and Andrew got everything plugged into her blog, they were definitely going to need some extra help especially with bridal registration and taking orders. None of them would be bored around there much longer.

If this promotion took off like she thought it would, it was going to be a madhouse around there. The first thing would be to post pictures of Andrew and her together and lay out the promotional pitch he did today. He really had his ideas well thought out and well put together, and you could tell that it came from the heart of a man in love. The couples who reached out to them on her blog would pick up on that.

Sharon silently scolded herself, "You really need to snap out of this daydream you are caught up in and try to stay focused." She had to take a break. It would do her some good to get out of the office for a while. It was already 2:00 p.m., and by the time she got back, she would only have a couple of hours left. When she got up front, Chrystal still was not back. She really couldn't believe Chrystal. Her attitude had been so weird since her visit with Andrew, and the way Dr. Robinson came across today didn't help.

Sharon couldn't put her finger on exactly what it was, but she was beginning to get very uncomfortable with the way Chrystal had been behaving lately. Sharon was not a spiteful person and even though she knew that the animosity from Chrystal was directed towards her, she really liked Chrystal and was willing to try again to make her feel valued. With Chrystal being gone over two hours on her lunch break, it seemed as if she was trying to pull Sharon into a confrontation with her.

Just as Sharon turned to go back to her office, Chrystal walked in. "I got hung up in traffic," she said nonchalantly.

"That's fine," Sharon said. "I'm wondering if we might get together and bounce some ideas around and talk about some things you might like to work on."

"Not really. It looks like you and Anne, oh, I forgot, it's Andrew now, have a monopoly on that already."

Sharon was livid. "Chrystal, I'm only going to ask you one more time, what's wrong?"

"Nothing. Whatever floats your boat, I guess. But with all you got going on for yourself, Sharon, why would you want to waste your time on Andrew? That's a joke."

When Sharon finally got over the astonishment of Chrystal's statements, she asked, "Chrystal, have you ever been in love with anyone besides yourself?"

"Well, I'm just saying," Chrystal said in a really rude fashion. From that moment on, Sharon knew it would be impossible for her to work with Chrystal. A team player she was not.

Sharon said, "Chrystal I'm going out for a while," and turned her back and walked away. When Sharon got to her car, she was so mad she could hardly control herself, and she didn't like the feeling. How could Chrystal be so cruel and not be able to see Andrew for the beautiful soul that he is? How could she not have some compassion for this person who has endured so much. Sharon didn't know how she would ever be able to work with Chrystal after today. She was miserable and didn't know how she would get past this before going home to Dru. It wouldn't take long for him to know something was wrong. That's just the way he was.

As she sat there in the car, she began to reflect back on the cruel and inhumane way Andrew's mother had belittled him that day, stripping him of his manhood and making life unbearable for him for over half of his life. Sharon just wanted to go home. She didn't want to be in the same room with Chrystal, and she needed to get a serious attitude adjustment before she went home to Dru. When she walked into her department leading to her office, she didn't look in Chrystal's direction.

"Sharon." Hearing Dr. Robinson's voice startled her, and she jumped. "Dr. Robinson, oh my goodness. I'm sorry," she managed to say. The last thing she needed was for Dr. Robinson to show up down there to an empty office, she thought to herself. "Is Chrystal not here?" she asked, her voice trembling. Just the thought gave her a headache.

Dr. Robinson directed her to a seat. "Sharon, let's

sit down for a minute," he said softly, and took her hand in his. "I heard everything Chrystal said to you earlier." It was like someone had knocked the breath out of her, and she could hardly speak.

"I went down to Louise's office to see if she could take a quick thirty-minute break to come down with me to your office so I could decide who would be doing what so you all would be on the same page, and that's when we heard the whole conversation between you and Chrystal."

"Dr. Robinson, I am so sorry," Sharon said. "I have done everything I know to do to make Chrystal feel valued, but what she said today and the way she said it about someone I love so dearly was infuriating. I must confess to you that I have never felt about anyone the way I feel about Andrew, and my love for him has been deep and silent for a very long time. We have recently begun to acknowledge this to ourselves. Andrew is just beginning to accept himself as a real person, and for her to speak about him the way she did today, stirred disturbing emotions within me. Just imagine if she had said that to him directly, doctor, or he had walked in and overheard that disgusting scene today. I am livid about it," Sharon confessed.

Dr. Robinson said nothing. He sat and held Sharon's hand and listened. She composed herself and spoke again. "Dr. Robinson, please don't terminate Chrystal, though. Please don't. I don't think I could live with myself if you were to do that."

He laughed softly. "Sharon, I knew you would say that, and no, I'm not going to terminate Chrystal, but I am going to move her to my department so I can keep an eye on her. Something wounding has happened in Chrystal's life, and it's left her bitter. Even though she has potential, it's something about you that makes her feel inadequate. I have given Chrystal the rest of the week off, and she will report to my department starting Monday."

He sat quietly for a moment, and then continued, "Very few people ever find their true soul mates, but you and Andrew truly have. Will it be easy for the two of you? No, it won't, but know that you will always have my protection, always remember that."

After Dr. Robinson left, Sharon could hardly compose herself. The events of the day had left her filled with joy and excitement, anger and frustration all mixed up into one big headache. What was it about her that made Chrystal feel the way she did? Was it the feeling of inadequacy like Dr. Robinson suggested? Was it because of her accomplishments, or was it envy, or both?

Sharon reflected back to the statement Chrystal made, when she referred to Andrew as a joke. "With all you got going for yourself, Sharon." That statement said it all.

Sharon was distraught at this point. She noticed she had missed a call from Lou while she was talking to Dr. Robinson, but she would call her later. She had to get home to Dru. She should have been home by now, and he would be wondering.

24

By the time she pulled up into the drive at Haven House, she felt numb. Dru was sitting on the porch with a welcoming smile, it almost felt cruel to have to hurt him by telling him about Chrystal.

"Hi honey."

"Hey, back atcha," he said grinning.

"I hope you were able to come down off of that adrenaline rush after this morning and get some rest,"

Sharon said. She laughed as well and began to tell him how proud Dr. Robinson was of him and so was she.

"Dru, I'm so excited, Aren't you, honey?"

"Yes. I'm excited about us working together, but that's not what I want to talk about right now," he said. He took her by the hand, and they went inside.

"Is there something wrong?" Sharon asked.

"Yes, Sharon. Come and sit with me, honey. Louise called me today," and when he said that her eyes began to burn. "Lou told me what happened between you and Chrystal today and that she and Dr. Robinson overheard the whole conversation."

Sharon laid her head on Andrew's shoulder, and tears ran down her face, and so did his. He brushed her hair away from her face and kissed her ever so gently. He was hurting too.

"I'm sorry honey for ruining our evening," she managed to say. He whispered in her ear in his smooth sexy voice, "Don't talk Sharon, just feel." He lay her back on the sofa and slowly unfastened her skirt. He managed to pull her panties and skirt down over her hips while letting his hands caress her belly and thighs and linger ever so briefly around her vagina. His hands cast a warm glow over her body causing her to tremble. She tried to sit up, but she couldn't. She was completely under his spell. He picked her up in his arms like she was weightless and carried her to their bed. He laid down and had her sit on top, his eyes devouring her like a predator.

When he first attempted to enter her, it hurt, but he had her under his control. Her eyes wide open, locked into his. She felt like she was under some kind of hypnotic trance, never going too deep, but yet in that perfect place. She could feel it, and her knees locked against his hips like a vice, and her uterus started to convulse. The pleasure was so intense, she briefly lost consciousness, like someone had turned the lights out leaving her drained and confused. This had happened to her each time Dru made her reach a climax. When she awakened, she was snuggled down in bed with a soft cover wrapped around her body. When she looked out the window, it was almost sundown, and that warm glow was still there. She didn't want to move.

It was as if Dru could sense when she was awake. He came over to the bed and kissed her. He had an intense way of looking at her. He said, "Dinner is ready, are you hungry?"

"Yes. I missed lunch today, and I'm starving."

"Good, it's ready when you are, okay?"

She told him she would take a quick shower and would be right out. "Would you like some help?" he said. "No, thank you. Your help is dangerous," she replied back.

"Well, have it your way." He looked at her with a crushed look on his face. "Can I at least have a kiss?" he asked. She put her arms around him, and he messed with her hair. It was so weird how connected they were to each other. Sometimes she could tell when he was watching her even when she couldn't see him, and that's the same way he was looking at her now. She squirmed a little, and he loosened his embrace. "I will be done in no time," she said, and quickly headed to the shower. She shampooed her hair, towel dried it, and let it finish drying on its own.

"What are we having that smells so good?" she asked.

"Baked potatoes with real butter." Instead of sour cream, he used something else, but whatever it was, it was heavenly. They had fresh broccoli florets and baked chicken with some kind of sauce that was sinful. He had set the table, had candles and a beautiful centerpiece. He pulled out her chair. "Come and sit down, honey. I thought it would be nice to celebrate our new venture." He poured her a glass of wine. "Enjoy," he said. "I can't have any right now because of the medication, but I hope to have some soon." The evening was divine.

During dinner, he showed her a couple of photos of them together that would be fantastic for the promotion and asked her opinion. "Dru, these are perfect. In fact, I have been looking for these. Where did you find them? she asked.

"I packed them when I was clearing out your apartment for the move."

"After dinner, let's post them along with the presentation you gave earlier in the day," she suggested. "This is on point, Dru," she said. "I could feel the love and sincerity today during your presentation, and I especially loved the part about us having the same last name - 'Now ladies, she won't even have to change her last name when he marries her.' "How perfect is that?"

Just hearing her laugh filled Dru with this wonderful feeling of satisfaction. "We don't need to change a thing," she said. Sharon further suggested, "If we get everything completed tonight, it will be ready for viewing first thing in the morning, and I can't wait to see how things will be going by the end of the day. My only concern is whether the site will be ready to take orders, and what about bridle registration?" she asked with a slight concern.

"Damn, Honey. What if customers start trying to place orders as soon as the site is up? Shit, we might be able to handle some of it on our end, but you and Louise could be in a real mess with only the two of you. I don't want things to get out of hand and then have to shut down the site."

"No way will I let that happen," he stated emphatically, and he meant it.

"No way are you going to start missing therapy," Sharon said, and she meant that too. "Missing therapy was not an option."

Sharon knew where Dru's head was at, but missing therapy was not up for discussion. When they finally finished everything up, it was late. They wanted things to be just so, and that was something else she had always noticed about them. They were true perfectionists. If things weren't just right, they would do it over until they were.

At last, Sharon couldn't stay up any longer. She was exhausted, and if she didn't get to bed soon, she wouldn't be worth a hill of beans in the morning. She worried about Dru.

He was starting to overdo things already, especially with the love making, but if he thought he was going to start slacking here and there on his rehab program, he was sadly mistaken. She wouldn't begin to let him start neglecting himself.

When she awakened, she felt tired and groggy. She hadn't slept very long at all. She quietly got out of bed and headed to the shower. She didn't want to wake Dru because he really needed to rest. She dressed quickly and was out of the house in short order, and by the time she got to The Company, she felt better.

Of course, Louise was already there. "Hi Lou. Sorry I didn't get back to you last night," Sharon told her. She thanked Lou for giving Dru the heads up about Chrystal yesterday. "I truly didn't know how I was going to be able to start the dialogue with that one," Sharon admitted. "Dru always has a way of making me feel better."

"I know he does!" Lou said with a laugh which in turn, brought a big grin to Sharon's face.

I don't know what I would do if I didn't have you as a friend," she told Louise. "When I'm floundering, you seem to always know how to help and with me not even having to ask. I will be so glad when you officially move down here permanently," she told her.

"Well as of today, I am officially all yours."

"What?"

"Yep, Dr. Robinson called me this morning. Said they found a replacement for my position and promised me I would be pleased with the final candidate." Sharon was so happy.

"Dr. Robinson is the greatest, Lou, don't you think?" Sharon asked, and Lou couldn't have agreed more.

"You do know he is moving Chrystal, don't you?" Lou continued.

"Yes, he told me yesterday." Sharon paused, and then asked the one question that puzzled her the most. "Louise, why do you think Chrystal has so much animosity towards me?" Louise could hear the sorrow in Sharon's words and as much as she wanted to give Sharon some consolation, she really didn't know herself.

"Women like Chrystal have a real problem with women like you, Sharon."

"Louise, that's exactly what Dr. Robinson said yesterday, but why Lou?"

"I don't know, and I don't think Chrystal really knows herself, at least to be able to put it into some perspective." "Lou continued, "Sharon for one thing, you're not fake. You genuinely care about other people. You are also beautiful, not just on the outside, but on the inside as well. Let me ask you something. Why do you think Andrew loves you so much?" That question left Sharon puzzled. "It's because having a woman like you who actually views him as the beautiful soul that he truly is and loves him unconditionally. Sharon, you're every man's dream."

Sharon thought for a minute. Now she was

beginning to get a sense of where Chrystal was coming from yesterday. Lou, I recall Chrystal saying, "Why would a woman like you waste your time with someone like Anne? Oh, excuse me, its Andrew now." It wasn't Andrew per se. Chrystal's attack was actually directed towards me, and Andrew was just how she felt about him, a joke. Do you remember that Lou?"

"I will never forget, and neither will Dr. Robinson, but Sharon, let me leave you with this one thought. You take things to heart, especially when you feel you have done something to hurt someone. Then you will go out of your way to fix it. Please don't let anyone ever change you. People like you are few and far between. Most people think about self-first and everyone else as an afterthought. Chrystal Johnson is a perfect example."

25

The weeks that followed were successful but overwhelming. Andrew did miss a couple of sessions with his therapist but seemed to be as fit as ever. Dr. Robinson was able to get help from another department until Andrew was released to return to work full time. He continued to accept applications for help hoping to fill positions before Dru's return.

Christopher, from advertising, is a seasoned employee that has been with The Company for twelve years and knows advertising like the back of his hand. He is thirty-seven years old and never married. He attended college and is a very nice person. Travis, a new trainee from creative arts, is young and eager to learn all aspects of the business and follows instructions well.

Dr. Clarke said Andrew could come back before the drawing for the cruise, so the extra people were a blessing, but by the end of the days that followed, everyone was exhausted. When Sharon got home each day, all she wanted to do was crash, and she hated it. Sometimes Dru would have to insist that she eat something before he would let her go to sleep.

They also decided to postpone the wedding until after the drawing for the trip. It wasn't something they wanted to do, nor would Dr. Robinson make them feel like it was something they should do, but The Company blog was as hot as a firecracker on the fourth of July. They were replete with last-minute entries trying to meet the deadlines along with registry orders through the roof.

"Good morning, everyone."

"Good morning, Louise and happy birthday," announced Christopher. Louise was already busy at work, and it was barely 8:00 a.m. "Thank God it's Friday," Christopher bellowed, finally getting Lou's attention.

"What?" When Lou eventually looked up and saw Christopher standing right in front of her desk holding the most beautiful flowers Lou had ever laid her eyes upon, she couldn't believe what she was seeing. "Happy birthday," Christopher said again.

"Oh, my goodness!" Lou exclaimed, clasping her hand over her mouth. Louise had completely forgotten her own birthday. "How did you know?" Lou asked when she got over the initial astonishment. Now that Christopher had her attention, it was obvious that he was enjoying every minute of it.

"I'll never tell," he said with a smile.

"Before we get too busy," he continued, "I wanted to ask if you would consider dinner and a late movie with me this evening? I know it's short notice, but things have been so hectic around here lately," he said. Louise was completely caught off guard.

"Before you tell me no, I was going to ask Sharon and Dru if they would consider accompanying us if it would make you feel more comfortable," he negotiated.

When Lou managed to find her voice, she replied, "Chris, thank you so much, and it's not that I don't trust you or anything like that, but I believe it would be a nice evening for all of us, if you don't mind."

Chris spoke up immediately, "Sharon, do you think Andrew would feel up to it, he asked?"

"I'll ask him, but I'm pretty sure it would be a welcomed evening for both of us." Christopher was ecstatic. "Well Lou, is that a yes?"

"Yes Chris, I would love that very much."

"Great! My treat, Sharon. Let Andrew know. Okay ladies, just so you know, I love scary movies. There is a new release I'm dying to see."

Sharon looked at Louise, and a gigantic grin came on their faces.

What?" Chris said.

"Chris, Louise and I love scary movies and the scarier the better. When Christopher and Louise looked at each other, it was clear, the magic was there.

"I'll call Dru," Sharon said, "I'm sure you can count on us." It was like someone had lit a fire under all of them, and when Sharon talked to Dru, naturally he was excited as well.

"Honey, tell Chris we would love to join them this evening, and since we are so far out, maybe we could meet them wherever they would be dining."

"I will let them know," she told him, "And if I can, I will try to leave around 5:00. Okay, honey?"

See you soon," Andrew said.

Sharon couldn't remember the last time they had been on an evening out. They had been so caught up in work. The rest of the day went by like a blur, and Sharon almost forgot to tell Chris what Dru suggested about meeting them where they would be having dinner. "Where were we going?" she asked.

"You ladies pick," he said.

Lou suggested Houston's since it was close to downtown and the theaters too. "Okay, Houston's it is," Chris said excitedly. Louise could see how much this evening meant to him. "Would 8:00 p.m. be good for everyone?" Chris asked. That will be fine, they all agreed.

"Great. Louise, I will pick you up around 7:30. All I need is your address and everything is all set. Well ladies, I am going to get out of here a little early so I can make reservations for the four of us and take care of some last-minute details. I will see you soon." Sharon knew that this was only the beginning for Louise and Christopher. She could feel it in her heart.

After Chris left, Louise didn't want to think beyond this evening, and when Sharon asked her if she had any idea Chris was interested, she indicated that she kind of did. At first, she just thought he was being a flirt. After today, she sensed it was much more.

Sharon asked Lou how she felt about this new revelation. "All of this is so new to me," she said, "And I have to admit, I'm a bit scared. Even though I know it would be a mistake not trusting my heart, I probably would have told him no without everyone's support."

"I could tell by the way he looked at you today that he wants a real relationship with you, but you seem scared," Sharon continued.

"What do you think, Sharon?" she asked, looking for Sharon's approval.

Sharon did not hesitate with her opinion, "Louise, it would be a mistake to not let your heart guide you."

Louise paused for a moment. She didn't mention it to Sharon before, but this was not the first time Christopher tried to talk to her, and she brushed him off.

"Louise, when was this?" Sharon asked.

"About a year ago. I was somewhere, I can't remember where, and Christopher came over to me and started talking to me as if he knew me forever. It felt right then, but when he asked if he could see me again, I wasn't ready. When he asked if he could call me some time, I never gave him my number, and I don't really know what happened after that. We just lost contact. After he got pulled down here to work a few weeks ago, I began to wonder if he remembered me, and it's obvious now that he does."

If Sharon had any doubts in her heart now, she didn't anymore. "Please don't push him away from you this time, Lou."

"I won't, I promise," Lou responded. "Let's get out of here," Lou said. "We have dates tonight."

When Sharon got home to Dru, the weekend seemed to take on a special meaning. This was something they all needed, and when Sharon told Dru about Christopher Alexander, he was thrilled for Lou. "Sharon, you are a good judge of people," he said. "You don't think Louise could get hurt in this relationship, do you honey?" he asked, concerned.

"No, I don't think so. I can see the way he feels

about Lou, and Louise told me today this was not the first time Chris had tried to talk to her. About a year ago, they were somewhere, and he came over and started talking to her like he knew her forever. Lou said it felt right then, but during that time in her life, she was very insecure and afraid of commitment. She probably would have said no today if she hadn't had our support."

"Honey, I asked Lou to please be open this time, but she is so unsure of herself. Remember how it was with us, Dru?"

How could I forget?" he replied. "I wanted to be with you so bad Sharon, but my demons were driving me to the brink of insanity. Your love is what saved me, and it still does today. You know I love you Sharon, but if you knew how much, it would probably blow your mind."

Sharon moved closer to him and nuzzled her face against his neck. "Andrew honey, I do know. I can feel it every time you touch me and in the way you look at me. I can see it in Christopher and Lou. They belong together, Dru. The wait is finally over for both. Is it scary? Sure, it is, but is it worth it? You bet it is, and I'm going to make sure that Louise takes the risk this time."

When Sharon finished getting dressed, Andrew was patiently waiting in the living room. "You take my breath away," he told her. "Can I hold you for just a little while?" She curled up in his lap. Never had she felt such complete contentment in her life until Dru.

"Honey, we have to get back on track with the

wedding," he said. "It seems like it has not been a priority with us lately, and it scares me."

"I feel the same way," she agreed.

Andrew was worried about Sharon lately. It wasn't something he could put his finger on exactly, but worried, nonetheless. "Honey, is everything okay with you?" he asked. She knew he had been worried.

"As I think back, there was a time when The Company was the most important thing in the world to me. Being in the limelight and being praised by Dr. Robinson was what I craved more than anything, but not anymore. I miss the closeness between us," she said. "Maybe it's because you aren't at work right now, and I miss you very much. When I'm at home with you like this, lately I've craved it more and more. I don't quite know when it all began, the feeling of being off somehow. Maybe once you return to work, I will feel okay, more complete."

"Hearing Sharon express her woes disturbed Andrew. He could feel something was happening with her, but the not knowing is what worried him even more. He tried not to dwell on it because he never wanted to take any of that away from her, but he knew something was wrong, he just didn't know what. "You've lost so much weight, for one thing honey, and I hate it when you come home exhausted every day. Monday, I'm going to have a long talk with Dr. Clarke. It's only two weeks before I'm to be officially released, and I'm going to ask him if I can come back a week early so I can keep an eye on you."

"I'm sorry," she apologized. "I don't know myself what is going on with me. I feel so weird lately, and a lot of it probably has to do with everything we have been through finally catching up to me." Being snuggled down in Dru's arms made her feel secure, and she didn't want to move. Sharon sighed and told Dru that it would make her happy if Dr. Clarke were to release him early. "Only if Dr. Clarke feels you are ready, honey, okay?" It was her insecurities showing and she looked into his eyes and smiled. These next two weeks would go by before they knew it.

Andrew didn't say anything else. He held out his hand to her. "We have a date, remember Mrs. Grayson?" This night out is exactly what they needed, and that was to stay focused on what was most important, and that was them. When they got to Houston's, Chris and Louise were already there. "Hey guys, it's about time you got here," Chris said. "Come and sit down."

"Lou, you looked so pretty," Sharon told her. Lou had on a blue dress that complimented her body beautifully. It made Sharon feel good to see Lou happy, and Chris as well.

"Sharon, let's dance," Andrew said. At that moment, she realized that they had never danced together. When Dru took her in his arms, her body melted into his. It almost felt like making love. The evening was marvelous, and Louise and Chris seemed to be in a world of their own.

Louise picked a wonderful place for dinner. They had been there before, but only for lunch. The evening had a completely different ambiance, and the food and the service were impeccable. The four friends spending time together seemed so right.

By the time they got to the theater, it was already crowded, but they still managed to get good seats. Christopher was right. The movie he suggested kept them on the edge of their seats the whole evening, and Sharon was practically in Dru's lap the entire time. Sharon caught a glimpse of Chris kissing Lou, and she didn't deny him. The whole evening was perfect.

By the time the movie was over, it was after midnight. Sharon was wide awake and feeling her old self again. "Dru, Sharon, thank you guys so much for coming out with us this evening," Chris said. "We will have to do this again and soon," they all agreed.

"How about next weekend? You guys should come out to Haven House for Sunday dinner," Andrew suggested.

"Honey, that's a great idea," Sharon agreed. "We'll talk about it next week." Chris held Lou's hand the whole time.

"See you Monday," Lou said.

"The whole evening was fabulous, wasn't it, Dru?"

"Yes it was, and I can see how comfortable Chris and Lou were with each other," Dru replied. Sharon was glad Dru could see it too.

When Sharon woke up on Saturday morning, Andrew was already up. "Good morning, sleepy head," Dru joked. "Did you sleep well?"

"Yes, honey, I did, but my body feels so strange."

"Well, today we're just going to relax and spend the day being lazy," Dru said. There would be no thinking about The Company, the promotion, the deadlines, or anything that had to do with work. "We will have enough of that to deal with on Monday. That's for certain with all the last-minute stuff to do, the last-minute entries, and everyone trying to get on the bandwagon, "Don't you mean the cruise ship," Andrew said.

"Okay, Mr. Smart ass," she said, and they both laughed. "Well, we only have two more days before the deadline, and I'm really glad about that." Sharon continued, "Honey, I had no idea this promotion would be so successful, and the eight-day cruise is motivation in itself." Dru could see where this was headed, and he tried to nip it in the bud.

"I'm going to start brunch," Dru said. "When it's done, I'm going to insist that you eat."

"What time is it?" she asked.

"It's 11:00."

"No wonder you called me sleepy head earlier."

"Sharon, please try to relax." She could tell he was getting irritated with her. "I mean it, Sharon," he said. "I don't like the way you have been feeling lately." He was fixing ham and cheese omelets, buttered toast with strawberry preserves and orange juice.

It wasn't like her to sleep so late. "Since it's so late, why don't we wait and have a nice dinner instead?" She dared not tell him she was not hungry. He didn't say much, except for her to relax, and he would bring her some orange juice.

"Thanks honey," she said.

It felt nice to just lay there and not have to move, she thought to herself. Maybe she needed to start taking a really good vitamin supplement since she has been eating so poorly. "Last night, being out with Lou and Chris was so nice," Sharon reminisced. Doing the things that normal people do took on a new meaning to Sharon. Everyone has to work, she realized that. But the day comes when you wake up and realize that the important things in life, like being in love with someone and having that person love you back so strongly that you can feel it deep down in your soul, becomes more of a priority.

Sharon had accomplished a great deal in the last few years at The Company, and until she met Andrew, her career was the focus of the majority of her attention, and that was all that mattered to her. Sharon realized that she had been missing out on so much more. When it came to Dru, all he ever had in his life was pain, suffering, and despair until a year ago. For over twenty-seven years, The Company was his lifeline as well. There was no outside life away from The Company, no family, just The Company, and now that they had found each other, suddenly there was a brand-new life to be discovered together.

Watching Louise and Christopher together last evening caused her heart to overflow, and she now understood that when that special person finally comes into your life, everything else just makes sense. When she opened her eyes, her warrior was standing there with a breakfast tray in his hands, just watching her.

"Hey, Ms. Lazy Bones, lunch is ready."

"Lunch? You're kidding, right?"

He smiled. "Would I lie to you, Mrs. Grayson?"

Boy, she had really been a space cadet today, she thought to herself. The look Andrew gave her let her know she had better eat or else.

"I made it simple," he said. "Now be careful, it's hot just like you like it. Cream of potato soup, homemade, of course." She sat up in the bed, and he sat down beside her. For what seemed like a long time, they didn't say anything. Finally, he asked, "Honey, what are you thinking about?"

"Oh, my recurring insecurities are visiting me once more," she said. "Will you promise me something, Dru? Promise me that you won't ever leave me again," she said quietly.

He messed with her hair like he always did. "What makes you think that I would ever do that Sharon? Talk to me, please, honey."

"The time in the hospital when you tried to drive me away from you. I was so scared, Dru. You didn't even want to come back to Haven House with me. I cannot bear the thought of living my life without you."

He lay beside her and held her in his arms. "Sharon, after making love to you, the thought of never getting that feeling back again almost drove me crazy. I know it wasn't just about the physical act itself, but also the emotions that go along with it. The way you looked and the control I had over those emotions and the outcome. Never would I ever be able to live without that again, nor would I allow you to. That night in the hospital, I watched you after you got out of the shower, and that's when I knew that all of those feelings that make me a man were still there. I would never have had that without you. We belong together, Sharon, and I will never let you go."

She snuggled down under his arm, and all was well in her soul. They laid together that way for quite some time and at first, she thought he had fallen asleep. Then out of nowhere he said, "Honey, let's go out and spend some money. We haven't done that, well…ever."

Sharon humorously pushed back and said, "Except when you went out and spent over three grand on this ring and we still haven't made our union legal yet."

He looked at her with his sexy smile and spoke, "Yeah, but that doesn't count. Well, it's either get out and go shopping, or…" He started crawling up the foot of the bed like a predator stalking its prey. Sharon laid back and stretched her arms up above her head while he crept closer and closer. She could feel his hot breath between her thighs. She jumped up and leaped out of the bed so fast.

"Okay, I give. Shopping it is," she said almost breathless.

"Shopping it is." He grabbed her and locked her in his embrace, laughing like they had everything they needed and nothing else mattered.

"Okay, Mrs. Grayson. I'm giving you fifteen minutes to get dressed. I'll be back."

"Okay, okay, I'm up," she said. She felt rested but not rested enough for Dru to make love to her. She definitely wouldn't have won that battle. Sometimes, she swore he drugged her in some way. Just that brief encounter had her under his spell, and she loved every minute of it.

After she got herself together and went out into the living area, he was sitting there waiting patiently. "Let's go warrior, or should I say, predator?"

"A little of both," he said and winked.

26

They went into the city and spent the entire evening. They had dinner at a wonderful Italian restaurant and bought clothes they didn't need and modeled for each other. Andrew bought two pairs of slacks for work, and they fit him perfectly. His body had changed so much throughout the year. The medicine Dr. Avery prescribed, along with therapy and weight training, left his body lean and toned with much definition. His bittersweet chocolate skin and his pearly white teeth made him what women would refer to as eye candy.

Next, it was her turn. She let Andrew choose what he wanted to see her in. They were having so much fun, and Dru had excellent taste in styles. It didn't take long for Sharon to realize that she had lost a whole dress size. She couldn't remember the last time she wore a size six. No wonder Dru had such control over her body, but really, he always had it anyway.

They had the same taste in clothing, and he loved it when she wore dresses. He picked two that she would have picked herself. When she put the first one on, it was a size seven-eight. "Honey, come out where I can see you," he requested. "You're going to need a six. He could look at her with such intensity at times, but he never pushed the issue. He went over and found it in a size six and the other one in a five-six. She tried the five-six on first, and when she went out, she didn't need any words. His eyes said it all.

"You like it?" she asked?

"I do," he said. They were so lost in the moment; they didn't notice the couple walking toward them until they spoke.

"Hi, Sharon and Andrew. We're John and Lucille Baker."

"Hey guys, how are you?"

"We just wanted to let you know that now, seeing the two of you together, how much in love the two of you really are, and that the promotion is not merely a pitch as a way of driving up sales. We signed up for the bridal registry and the chance to win the cruise, which is probably a million to one shot, but just watching the two of you together, feeling the way you do about each other; it just shows." John shook Dru's hand, and Lucille hugged Sharon.

"Thank you guys so much for coming over and talking to us," Andrew said. "Meeting you one on one makes us feel more connected as well. Unfortunately, we don't get to pick the winning couple," Sharon continued, "Or I'd wind up with a runner up and a second runner up," and they all laughed.

"We won't hold you up any longer," Lucille said. "Enjoy the rest of your day."

"Good luck on the trip," Andrew said. Sharon went back into the dressing room to change her clothes. Lucille and John coming up and introducing themselves was great. Dru took Sharon in his arms and kissed her. "Are you ready to go home, Mrs. Grayson?"

"I'm ready when you are, Mr. Grayson."

"This has been the most fabulous weekend. We're going to have to do things like this more often," Dru said.

"We've lost out on so much, especially you," Andrew," Sharon said. It hurt her every time she thought about how much he had been through.

"Sharon, can I hold you, just for a little while longer?" and she could feel how much the past had affected Andrew and still did.

The next morning after breakfast, they briefly visited The Company blog to see what they had been waiting for them the following morning, and it was pretty much what they had expected. They would deal with it when the time came because the rest of the weekend belonged to them.

"Good morning, everyone."

"Good morning," Louise responded back. Sharon was anxious to talk to Lou. She hadn't spoken to her since their awesome Friday night double date. Sharon went over and hugged Lou from the back and whispered in her ear, "Please tell me that things are still perfect."

"Better than perfect," Lou said. Sharon looked over at Chris and it was clear that all was well with the two of them. Poor Travis was already up to his neck filling orders.

The phone rang, "Good morning, Sharon Grayson. May I help you?"

"Good morning, Sharon. How are you this morning?"

"Well, doctor."

"Good, I will see you soon."

"Everyone, Dr. Robinson is on his way and as soon as he gets here, he wants to have a brief meeting with us." She immediately got Andrew on the line so he could listen in. "Hi honey, Dr. Robinson is on his way and as soon as he gets here, I'll be calling you back."

"Okay, honey." He had a pretty good idea what he wanted to talk about, and that was bringing in some new people because the next couple of days were going to be rough.

Sharon sat down at her computer and pulled up The Company blog. It was worse than she imagined. "Good morning, everyone."

"Good morning, Dr. Robinson." Sharon got Andrew on the line.

I'm sure by now everyone is aware that we desperately need a couple of new people. The only problem is whomever we get, they won't have a clue about what's going on. Christopher immediately spoke up. "Dr. Robinson, "I'm already down here on a temp basis. Before you take on any new employees, can I put in a verbal request right now for a permanent transfer?"

"Well, Chris, that would be a tremendous loss for advertising, but if you're sure that's what you want, I'm sure Sharon and Louise would love to have you. Andrew, are you there?"

"Yes, Dr. Robinson."

"Guys, how does everyone feel about Chris coming on board?"

"Welcome to the team Christopher," they all said in

unison.

"Well, that's that, " Dr. Robinson said. "Things may be a little hectic for you because I'd like for you to help out advertising by training the new person, but consider this position yours. Please submit a written request to me as soon as possible. Now, if anyone has any ideas how we can get through these next few days without having a nervous breakdown, I would love to hear it."

"Dr. Robinson, I just got off of the phone with Dr. Clarke, and he has agreed to release me as of today," Andrew said. Sharon's heart caught in her throat.

"Oh, Dru, man, that's great! These women are conspiring against us around here," Chris said. "Tell me about it, Chris," Dr. Robinson chimed in.

"Sharon had the nerve to try and use my own expertise against me a few days ago by saying, and I quote: "Oh, Dr. Robinson, Louise and I would just love it if you would come down and work with us, just until Andrew comes back," Dr. Robinson chided. Andrew, I think they are trying to send me out on an early retirement.

" Sharon laughed so hard; her head hurt.

"Dr. Robinson and Chris, just hold on, " Andrew said, trying to keep from choking, he was laughing so hard! "Warrior is on his way. "See you soon.

Everyone was extremely happy, but most of all Sharon.

BOOK TITLE

"Dr. Robinson, I would like to wait until Andrew gets here to make a final decision "Lou said but If the five of them can come to an agreement, we could all take a small break after work and come back and work until 10:00 p.m. for the next few nights because trying to train someone new would only be a hindrance," Louise suggested."

How do you feel about that Sharon?" Dr. Robinson asked.

"Well guys, I agree with Louise. That's about the only way we are going to pull this off," Sharon responded.

"We will only have four nights to pull this off because Travis has school," Dr. Robinson reminded them. Sharon assured Travis that would not be a problem. They were there to support each other.

"Thanks Sharon, but you guys know that I will be here the next two evenings," Travis replied.

"It looks like we have a plan," Dr. Robinson said, "And you know that you will be well- compensated for all of your hard work. And Sharon, as soon as you talk it over with Andrew, just let me know."

"I will, doctor, and we'll talk soon."

After Dr. Robinson left, Chris went over and stood in front of Lou's desk. He looked deeply into her eyes. "Louise, you don't think I'm pushing you too fast, do you?" he asked, almost holding his breath. "If you do, just tell me and I will back off, but this time, please know I will never back away. I don't want to lose you again like I did the last time," he said, keeping his voice low. She reached across her desk and touched his hand, and he smiled.

"Hey, Dru." When Andrew walked in, his eyes locked with Sharon's, and his being there was all the support she would need. "It's so good to have you back," they all said. Travis introduced himself.

"Well, where do we start?" Andrew asked, never taking his eyes off of Sharon.

"Dru, before you got here, Lou came up with a suggestion she wanted to run by you."

Okay Lou, what's up?"

I suggested that at about 5:00 p.m., we could take a short break and come back and work until 10:00 p.m. This would be for the next two evenings, but we wanted to wait until you got here before deciding." His eyes immediately went back to Sharon. "Sharon, is that okay with you," he asked?

"Yes, with you here, we could pull it off," She could see the concern in his eyes. Under his breath, so no one could hear, he asked, "Honey, are you sure?" Louise and Chris were hard at work, but she did see Louise look at Chris and smile.

Travis said, "Let's get this show on the road. I might have school tonight, but I want to get as much done as I can before I leave, and I will definitely be here for the next two days."

"That's a deal, Travis!" they all said.

By 5:00 p.m., Sharon was so weary she could hardly stay focused. If she could lay down just for a little while, maybe it would pass. Louise sensed that this was going to be a long evening for Sharon because she said, "Hey Dru, why don't you and Sharon take the first break, and Chris and I can take the second." Dru gave her the thumbs up.

"Hey honey, are you ready to get out of here for a while?" She didn't say anything, she merely smiled. He knew that another five hours were going to be more than she could handle.

When they got out to the car, Dru opened the door, and when she got in, he fastened her seat belt. "Let's go to Nanna's," she said. "That's closest." She took out her cell and called.

"Hi Nanna."

"Hi Darling. How are you guys doing? Busy, I'm sure."

"You guessed it, Nanna. Are you home?"

"Sure honey, come on by."

"Thanks Nanna, we're on our way."

They were both quiet during the drive over. Sharon knew that Dru had a lot on his mind. Finally, she broke the silence by saying, "After this is over, I'm going to make an appointment with Dr. Lakeland. Maybe she will prescribe a good vitamin supplement for me. It's because we have been so busy. After the promotion is over, I'm going to put in for a couple of extra days to extend into the weekend." Andrew didn't say anything, he just listened. Nanna was so glad to see them.

"Come on in," she said.

"I apologize for not coming sooner, but it's been like a madhouse around the studio lately," she told her.

"I know," Nanna said and smiled. "I remember you talking about the bridal promotion you have going on."

"Come, sit down, Andrew. It's good seeing you look so well," and he went over and gave Nanna a hug. Sharon curled up on the sofa. It felt so good for Sharon to relax her body just for a little while. Nanna lowered her voice, "Andrew, is everything alright with Sharon?" She was suddenly worried about her, and so was Dru.

"That's why I came back to work today," he told Nanna.

"She has lost so much weight," Nanna noticed. "She used to have such a healthy appetite."

"I'm going to make an appointment with Dr. Lakeland first thing in the morning. I'm not going to sit back and wait for Sharon to do it," Andrew insisted.

"Please do, Andrew." He could hear the concern in Nanna's voice.

"Don't worry, Nanna, I will." We are working until 10:00 p.m. tonight trying to meet the deadline. Tomorrow is our last day, and I'm so glad about that."

Nanna continued, "Sharon has always pushed herself. I hope she hasn't over done it this time. Andrew, please be watchful."

"Oh, Nanna, you already know," he said, comforting her.

"Sharon honey." She could hear Dru calling her name, but it sounded far away. She could feel him brushing her hair back away from her face like he always did.

"Sharon, you are so tired. Please let me take you home. I know Louise and Chris won't mind. In fact, you can continue to rest here with Nanna, and I can go back and help them finish."

That's a great idea," Nanna said. With that, Sharon sat up ready to go.

"No, I feel much better now that I had that power nap. I'm ready to roll, but Nanna, as soon as this is over, Andrew and I are coming over for Sunday dinner," she said, trying to change the subject.

"Of course, anytime. You know that, but please make it soon."

"I will, Nanna. I promise," Sharon confirmed.

Sharon wanted to go home in the worst way, but the sooner they got back, the sooner they would be done. When they walked into the studio, Louise was hard at work. "We're so glad to have you back, Andrew," she said. "Now it's just like old times."

"Me too, Lou," he said, "But more than anything, it is so good to see you so happy."

"Chris went to get carry out, but he will be back soon. We can share if you guys haven't eaten yet," Lou said knowing Sharon probably hadn't. After Sharon walked away, that made the perfect opportunity for Dru to let Louise know what his plans were. "Lou, before it gets any later, I'm going to put in a call to Dr. Lakeland and see if she can meet us at Emergency Medical."

Lou replied, "Good, I'm glad. Sharon thinks she's leaving us holding the bag with things being so critical right now. Don't let her get away with that, Dru. Something is wrong with Sharon." Andrew asked Lou to keep Sharon occupied while he made the call.

"Sharon let's look over these orders before I give them the okay," Lou suggested.

Sure, Lou."

Andrew was anxious, but more than anything else, worried. "Good evening, this is Dr. Lakeland. May I help you?"

"Yes, doctor." Andrew introduced himself and explained that he was calling in reference to one of her patients, Sharon Grayson.

"Yes? Is there something wrong with Sharon?"

"Dr. Lakeland, I know it is after hours, but if it's not

too much of an inconvenience, could you please meet us at Emergency Medical? Sharon has not been feeling well for a while now, and we have been so busy here at the studio. This has never been a problem before as she usually thrives on all of the excitement. Lately, she has been extremely tired, is losing weight, and is not her vibrant self anymore." Andrew continued, "We are engaged to be married, and I am very worried about her."

"Andrew, did you say your last name was Grayson, also?"

"Yes, doctor, but that's another story. If you could please check her out, it would help us rest a whole lot better tonight." He went on to explain that they have a small cottage several miles out of the city, and before he took her that distance, she really needed to be seen. "Even if you can't see her until tomorrow, if you could just order some labs or whatever, we would have an idea of what was going on with her."

Dr. Lakeland could tell how concerned Andrew was about Sharon and knew he had probably tried to get her to make this appointment herself, but she knew Sharon all too well. "Andrew, Emergency Medical is not out of my way at all and not an inconvenience," she assured him. "I will meet you there in forty-five minutes if that works for you."

"That would be perfect, doctor. See you soon."

Andrew's timing couldn't have been better. As soon as he ended the call, Sharon walked in. She went over and kissed him on the neck. "Honey, I wondered where you disappeared to. Is everything okay?"

"Everything's fine," he said lightly, "But will you come with me to run a few errands?"

"Sure."

"Lou, will you guys be okay until we get back?" she asked. "We have a few things to take care of."

"Sure. Take your time," Lou said.

"See you in a few," and they left.

When Sharon got into the car, it didn't take long for the weariness to engulf her, and she could hardly keep her eyes open. Riding in the car gave her body the chance to go back into shut-down mode.

"Sharon, come with me," she heard Andrew say. She opened her eyes a little.

"Honey, can't I just sit here until you get back? I will be fine." When she opened her eyes briefly, she had trouble comprehending where they were.

Dru came around and opened the door and helped her stand. The lights were so bright, and it reminded her of the night Andrew was shot. She heard someone ask if they needed help, and Andrew told them that his wife had not been feeling well. "Dr. Lakeland is her physician," he told them.

"Yes, Mr. Grayson, Dr. Lakeland has notified us that you were coming." Sharon was so confused.

"Dru, Honey?"

"Sharon, I'm not going to sit back and do nothing any longer. Dr. Lakeland feels you need to be seen and so do I. Maybe she can prescribe a good vitamin supplement just like you said so you can start feeling better. Don't you want to be feeling your best for our wedding?" he asked, trying to use reverse psychology.

With her tired eyes, she looked into his eyes and pleaded, "Dru, please don't be upset with me. How could you ever think that?"

"My beautiful, sweet wife."

"Mrs. Grayson?"

"Yes," Sharon responded back. The nurse escorted Sharon to an exam room, had her undress and put on a gown.

"Dr. Lakeland wants to keep you through the night so she can run a series of tests. She wants you to know that she will be here to discuss the results with the two of you first thing in the morning."

Now Sharon was scared, and so was Andrew. Sharon could see it in his eyes. She couldn't pretend to be okay any longer, and that's the part that scared her the most.

"After dinner, someone will be coming up from the lab to draw blood," the nurse said. Sharon dreaded the thought, but if that's what it took to find out what was wrong, that's all that mattered.

The nurse came in and brought her a menu and

asked Dru if he would like to have dinner with Sharon. He said he would. When they brought it up, she remembered what Andrew had said about hospital food, and now the shoe was on the other foot.

"Dru?"

"Yes, honey?"

"What do you think is wrong with me?" she asked.

"Extreme exhaustion, for one thing. It's probably the main thing, but you know honey, when we get past this, we are going to start doing things differently. No more pushing yourself to the extreme, Sharon. Life is too short for us to not be at peace with ourselves. We've had enough drama in our lives to last us a lifetime." Andrew went on to remind her of how much life they had missed out on and would never get back.

"We've missed out on dancing, going to the movies, shopping, and vacations. When is the last time you went on a vacation?" he asked. I have never been on a vacation in my entire life. These are the kinds of things people do every day that we know nothing about." Dru was so distraught at this point, and he tried not to upset Sharon any more than she already was. She knew that everything he was saying was true.

"Just try to rest, honey," he said. "You need that more than anything else," and he kissed her hand that he was holding in his. "Just know that whatever is going on with you, we will be dealing with it together."

That night was the longest night of their lives. Just a few weeks ago they were fighting for Andrew's life, but now Sharon was the only thing in the world that mattered to him. All he wanted was for her to be back to her old self again.

The next morning, the nurse came to check Sharon's vitals and Sharon asked her for some idea when Dr. Lakeland would be coming in. "I'm not sure, but most likely before 9:00 a.m. All of your lab results are in," she said.

Sharon was nervous, and she could tell Dru was like a powder keg trying not to blow up. She cupped his face in her hands and brushed her fingers across his brows telling him she felt better already. "I'm just overly tired," she told him. "Today is the last day of the promotion and with a good vitamin supplement and a couple of days off, I will be back to my old self."

He hoped so, and he couldn't wait for Dr. Lakeland to come. Sharon laid there thinking about what Lou and Chris must be going through. It was still fairly early, but she knew they would be in the studio earlier than usual and late again that night. That bothered Sharon. Finally, she said, "Honey, maybe we can go in around noon and at least help Chris and Lou try to finish up." Andrew immediately bulked at the idea.

"Sharon, please! Let's just wait until Dr. Lakeland comes in and we can go from there."

Sharon immediately backed off. "Okay, honey. Whatever Dr. Lakeland says I need to do, I will do."

At last, around 9:30 a.m., the nurse came in and advised that Dr. Lakeland was down the hall and would be coming in shortly. Sharon said, "I just want to know what is going on with me and fix it so I can start feeling better. It seems with the slightest exertion; it causes listlessness and lethargy to return. I hate it." She heard Dr. Lakeland talking to one of the nurses about her lab results. When she came in, she could tell how nervous they were. She introduced herself to Andrew and told him how happy she was to finally meet him.

"Periodically, I get the chance to keep up with Sharon on her blog, so I can see why she would be having some problems. It is so obvious that she has been over-extending herself."

"Sharon, you have extreme anemia, to the point of being dangerous. Under ordinary circumstances, a good vitamin supplement would help, but now I'm afraid it is more serious than that," Dr. Lakeland advised.

Dru was beside himself. "Oh my God, please!" Andrew exclaimed.

Dr. Lakeland could see how afraid they were. Their very lives were at stake because they were one. Sharon, she hadn't seen her for over six months or more.

"The last time I talked with you at length, you were adamant that the two of you did not want children. When did that change?" she asked. All of a sudden, Sharon was locked in fear.

"Dr. Lakeland, what are you trying to say?"

Sharon, you are three months pregnant."

Sharon was beside herself. "No, I'm not pregnant, Dr. Lakeland." Andrew was in shock.

"Have you been taking your birth control?" she asked Sharon, trying to calm the situation down, but Sharon couldn't think straight. Dr. Lakeland knew this was the last thing they expected to hear. "Sharon, your anemia can be extremely dangerous for you and the baby," Dr. Lakeland said.

"Dr. Lakeland, please," Sharon continued, practically grasping for straws. "But what about the weight loss? I don't feel pregnant."

"Sharon, actually you have been feeling pregnant, you just didn't make the connection. Has your body been feeling weird lately? More tired? Loss of appetite? The anemia only makes it worse."

She then turned to Andrew and addressed him. He seemed to be in a perplexed state of mind. "Andrew?"

"Yes?"

"Knowing that you were not planning on having children complicates this situation because with a sonogram, I can already inform you of what sex your child is. So, if there is even a remote possibility that you two are considering terminating this pregnancy...." Dr. Lakeland didn't want to continue with that thought but proceeded, "Just know that whatever you decide, it will have to be soon. Either way, your baby is in danger. Sharon, I will release you today; however, no matter what the decision is, I will still have to do everything medically necessary for the baby."

Right before Dr. Lakeland left the room, Andrew spoke up, "Dr, Lakeland, I want to know what the sex of my child is," and that is when Sharon was overcome with emotion. She began to cry uncontrollably. Dr. Lakeland closed the door and came over to Sharon. "Sharon, what about you? Do you wish to know as well?" Dr. Lakeland asked.

"Yes, I want to know as well."

"Okay, I will schedule you for a sonogram later this afternoon. I will not release you today, and you will have to begin treatment for the anemia. That has to get under control as soon as possible. You will be free to go home first thing in the morning. I will see you this afternoon for the sonogram."

When Dr. Lakeland left the room, they both were in disbelief. If Dr. Lakeland only knew how utterly impossible this should have been for Andrew because of his condition, she would have been mortified. Yet, it wasn't utterly impossible, after all. Both had overwhelming and confusing feelings going on inside of them, almost pulling them apart.

What was going to happen to this beautiful love affair between them? Would Andrew look at her differently now? Sharon was hurting. She laid back down on the bed and turned her back to Andrew. Never could she have imagined doing that, and he didn't say anything. The silence between them was like a death. How could she have let something like this happen to them? It has always been the two of them against this cruel world. All of a sudden, she heard Dru talking on his phone.

"Good morning. This is Anne Marie Peterson. May I please speak to Dr. Avery?"

Sharon thought she would never hear Andrew refer to himself that way ever again. Sharon immediately turned over and faced him, and she could feel a huge crack in her heart.

"Dr. Avery, it is imperative that I see you," she heard Andrew say. She could not hear what Dr. Avery was saying, but she did hear Andrew tell him that he was going to be a father. When her eyes connected with his, they both were looking for the answer that could change their lives, forever. Would they be terminating their baby's life or not? Sharon felt like her whole sanity would snap at any moment. Andrew came over to her and laid his ear against her belly and kept it there for a long time. He took Sharon in his arms, brushed her hair away from her face, and looked deeply into her eyes. "I love you Sharon with all that I am because that's all that you asked of me, no more, no less. And no, Sharon, we are not terminating our baby's life."

Sharon could hardly speak. "Please don't stop loving me because I let this happen, Dru. I never meant for this to happen." He looked at her intensely and when he spoke, he said, "Sharon, our baby is a boy."

"Andrew, how do you know that?" she asked,

completely caught off guard.

"I can't explain how I know; I just know. And Sharon, we're going to be a family." Sharon sobbed.

At that moment, an inner peace enveloped her, and it was like nothing she had ever felt in her life. All of her doubts, her fears, and her uncertainties seemed to melt away. There was a living, breathing life inside of her, a new beginning, and it felt so right. Sharon fell asleep and slept like she hadn't in months. When she opened her eyes, Andrew was still sitting beside her, watching. "Honey, the nurse is here to get you ready for the sonogram," he said softly. She brought in all of the equipment needed and transferred Sharon to a different bed.

"Dr. Lakeland is here, and there is no reason to be nervous," the nurse told her. Sharon laughed softly because it must have shown.

"What does the test do, exactly?" Andrew asked.

"A lot. It lets us know if the baby is developing normally, how much it weighs, and the baby's sex. It will also let us know if there are any abnormalities. Would you like to know the sex of your child?"

"Yes!" they both said at the same time.

"Great. The sonogram is painless. You won't have to worry about any discomfort." The nurse left the room to let Dr. Lakeland know they were ready.

BOOK TITLE

28

Sharon felt an inner calm that seemed to assuage her feelings of uncertainty and doubt that threatened her sanity a short time ago. It was surreal. That feeling came the moment they knew they were keeping their baby, and now it felt like a blessing that was overflowing through her body. She was certain it would never leave her. She had always felt Dru's love for her, but now, that same love had created an unbreakable bond between them that would survive all trials.

When Dr. Lakeland came in, the first thing Andrew said was, "Dr. Lakeland, we are keeping our baby." Dr. Lakeland was visibly moved by their decision. "Sharon, Andrew, as a professional, I have always been told to keep my personal feelings to myself, but your decision today has given me much joy. I have been a part of Sharon's life from the time she was a very young woman, and I care profoundly about her well-being. A very passionate love created the life inside you, Sharon, and that life deserves to live. Now, let's see what we've got going on in there," she said, and they all laughed with joy.

Dr. Lakeland warned Sharon that the lubricant she would be using on her belly would be cold and naturally, she was right. She used the wand to spread it around, and Sharon began to see a lot of weird movements going on. Andrew seemed to be in a trance. "There's a leg," Dr. Lakeland said.

"There's another leg and both arms. I see all ten fingers." She applied a little more lubricant, and then they heard a thumping sound. "What's that?" Andrew asked. "That's your baby's heartbeat, Andrew, and it is very strong," Dr. Lakeland replied.

All at once, Andrew jumped up out of his seat. "What's that?" Dr. Lakeland.

"Look closely and tell me. What do you think it is, Andrew?"

"Oh my God, Sharon. It's a boy! Our baby is a boy," Andrew cried out.

"Dr. Lakeland, earlier Dru said he our baby was a boy, and he was right," Sharon uttered.

"And he's perfect," Dr. Lakeland said, adding to their feeling of elation. Big tears began to flow from Andrew's eyes.

After Dr. Lakeland completed the exam, Andrew took Sharon in his arms, holding her close to his heart. She never wanted him to let her go.

"Well, Sharon and Andrew, baby Grayson seems to be doing quite well considering the anemia. I want you to take one more day off to regain your strength. When you do go back to work, please try to find some kind of balance with your hectic schedule until you go on maternity leave. It would be ideal if you could potentially be a stay-at-home mom for at least the first six months. For right now, I want you to come to see me twice a month, and I will be starting you on a good prenatal vitamin as well as something for the anemia."

"Thank you so much for everything, Dr. Lakeland," they both said. The awe she saw in their eyes was thanks enough.

"See the two of you in a couple of weeks," she said and left the two of them to relish in their joy.

Dr. Lakeland stuck her head back in the door and told them they had visitors. It was Christopher and Louise. Sharon could tell they were worried, but they hadn't gotten the chance to come up until now. Sharon noted how they looked so good together.

"Sharon, you look so much better," Lou said, and she was so relieved. "Yesterday, I could tell something was wrong.

"Yes, it was Lou, and it was a blessing that Dru brought me to the hospital when he did," she responded.

"Dr. Lakeland told me I have anemia, and that's why I felt so tired, plus the weight loss. But something else is complicating it even more."

Andrew looked at Sharon and he gave the okay. Chris had his arms around Lou, and they looked happy together.

"Before we tell you about this, we want you to keep this strictly between the four of us until we are ready to make it public."

"Now guys, you know we would never do anything to expose your privacy," Lou said.

"We know you won't, and that's why we want to share it with you. Andrew will burst if he doesn't share the wonderful news with you." Sharon paused. Andrew bellowed with pride and exclaimed, "Sharon is three months pregnant, and we are having a boy!"

Lou hollered with joy; she was beside herself. "I'm going to be a godmother, and one day I will have my own, and you can be Auntie Sharon!" Lou was suddenly embarrassed by the comments she had just blurted out, but to Chris, it seemed like the most logical response in the world.

"Lou, when the lab work came back and Dr. Lakeland told us we were going to be parents, you can only imagine the emotional upheaval we went through, especially when that was the last thing we expected to hear."

At that moment, the nurse stuck her head in the door and let them know that Dr. Robinson had left a message for the two of them. "He doesn't want either of you worrying about a thing. He wants you to concern yourselves with getting better, and he will be coming up this evening."

"Thank you so much," they both said.

Sharon asked Louise if the contest winners had been selected yet. "Not yet," she said. "The contest does not officially end until midnight tonight, and the drawing will be at noon the following day."

"Andrew, this promotion made big bucks for The

Company, but you definitely created a monster. You and Sharon are celebrities. I know Dr. Robinson is up to something, Sharon," Lou continued.

"Maybe I can get it out of him when he comes up here tonight," Sharon said. "Lou, as soon as the winning couple has been selected, please let us know."

"Without a doubt, "you know I will, Sharon."

"Dr. Lakeland told me I need to take one more day off, and I'm going to follow her instructions to the letter," Sharon went on.

"I don't blame you at all," Lou told her. "Anemia can be serious all by itself, but with that beautiful baby in the mix, taking chances is not an option."

"I love you Lou," Sharon told her, and that brought tears to Louise's eyes. "Can you imagine how excited Nanna will be when you guys tell her about the baby?" Lou beamed. Sharon smiled the biggest smile.

Lou sat on the side of the bed, holding Sharon's hand while Dru and Chris sat over in the corner relaxing and enjoying each other's company. "Andrew looks so complete and so happy," Lou said. "I would love to know what the two of them are talking about over there. Wouldn't you, Sharon?"

"Oh, I don't know about that, Lou. My ears are already burning," and they laughed so hard.

BOOK TITLE

BOOK TITLE

EPILOGUE

When Sharon looked around, she realized it didn't take much at all to make her feel complete. It's been said that as long as you have one or two true friends, that's all you'll ever need, and the rest are only acquaintances. That is so true.

Well, Sharon has been truly blessed with seven, each one coming into her life, just at the right time. Sharon has always believed that life and living is a process, and everyone in it has a special part, but it's the key players that leave a permanent mark on the heart that never goes away.

Dr. Robinson came through with flying colors. Sharon and Andrew's love for The Company and their years of dedication were never overlooked. Louise Russell, Christopher Alexander, and Andrew Grayson, Sharon's wonderful husband, together with Sharon, are currently laying on a beautiful beach in the Bahamas along with the winning couple that didn't win the contest. Yes, you heard right. Because Dr. Robinson loves Sharon so much, he lets Sharon pick a runner up and guess who she picked? You guessed it. The couple who came up to them that day in the dress shop, John and Lucille Baker.

The day Andrew and Sharon called them and invited them to come down to the studio, they couldn't understand what was going on because the winning couple had already been announced. When they walked into the studio, they were quite excited. "So, this is where it all happens," John said.

"Well, John and Lucille, I would first like to introduce you to the owner of The Company, Dr. Charles Robinson, and guess what? You are going on a cruise. Eight glorious days, all expenses paid along with the winning couple, Shelia and Anthony Gleason. Andrew and I, Louise and Christopher will be joining as well."

Everyone cheered. "So, get your bags packed and your relaxation on! Oh, and by the way, you are cordially invited to attend the wedding ceremony of Sharon and Andrew Grayson on Friday, August the 25th at Sundown on, a magnificently beautiful beach, in Belize, where we'll all create memories to last a lifetime."

Dr. Robinson just sat back and watched all of them. Making people happy has always done something to Sharon on the inside, and it's a feeling mere words cannot adequately express.

See you soon for Freak, A Love Story Part Two. I promise you won't be disappointed. If you enjoyed this read, please be so kind as to leave a review on Amazon.

ABOUT THE AUTHOR

A.L. Russell, was born in 1945, in Little Rock, Arkansas, home of the razorbacks, central high school, and the 42nd president of the United States- William J. Clinton. This is an exciting time in her life because this is her first time publishing her writing in the adult romance genre. She has always had a love for storytelling, finally after encouragement from her granddaughter, she decided to step out of her comfort zone and share her gift with the world. After more than a quarter of a century working at the Kansas Neurological Institute in Topeka, Kansas, Russell learned firsthand the power that unconditional love can have on an individual's mental health, which is the focus of her first novel, freak: a love story. Russell sites authors Nancy Giddeon and Sandra Brown as inspiration that keep the wild fires burning in her own daily life.

BOOK TITLE

Made in the USA
Columbia, SC
22 June 2023